EMILIA
Part One

THE TRASSATO CRIME FAMILY
Book #3

BY LISA CARDIFF

EMILIA

Limitless Publishing, LLC
Kailua, HI 96734
www.limitlesspublishing.com

Formatting: Limitless Publishing

ISBN-13: 978-1-64034-089-3
ISBN-10: 1-64034-089-0

CHAPTER ONE

Five years ago...

I flipped through page after page of paperwork in the file cabinet of my father's intricately carved wooden desk, looking for evidence that would set me free. My father, Dominick Trassato, was the head of the family and not in the *Leave it to Beaver* sort of way. He was the godfather, the don, the boss, or whatever else people called him, of the Trassato Crime Family, and I detested him as much as I loved him.

My feelings weren't always so convoluted. At one point, I would have professed to love him more than anyone in the world. Everything changed the night my mom died, though. She came home from a trip and they fought. From the banister overlooking the great room, I saw her smash framed pictures against the wall, throw pillows, and land punch after punch against my father's chest. My mom wanted to divorce him and move to Chicago to live with family friends while she restarted her career. My father put her on notice that the only way out of the marriage was death.

Apparently she took his threat literally because the sound of sirens and people running through my house jarred me awake a few hours later. My mom died from an overdose of sleeping pills in the bathtub, and my life as I had known it was over.

No more laughter, no more family trips, no more family dinners.

Even though my days of hero worship had ended, my father still lorded over me and everyone else in our insular world. He reminded me of the sun with everyone orbiting around him. He had charisma, charm, and an indescribable *something* that sucked people in and made them jump to do his bidding. Unlike everyone else, I refused to bend to his will. I knew his plans for me, and I intended to fight him every step of the way.

I dedicated my spare time to finding ways to blackmail my father until he agreed to set me free, and here I was years later sifting through his office papers, taking pictures of things I thought would be useful.

The cord to my headphones snagged on the corner of the desk, yanking them from my ears. An ominous noise replaced the soothing melody of the sonata I was learning to play for my next performance.

Tap. Shuffle. Click.

Footsteps. Lots of them clipped over the tiled hallway outside of the home office, edging closer and closer. A suffocating tightness clamped around my ribcage, and my entire body freeze-framed with my hand still inside my dad's filing cabinet. He told me he wouldn't be home until after I went to bed.

My gaze skittered around the room wildly searching for a hiding place. Every inanimate object shuffled through my brain. Desk. Chair. Plant. Bookshelf. Coat rack. And then I saw it—my father's built-in credenza. It spanned the front of his office beneath a wall of diamond shaped leaded glass windows overlooking our circular driveway now filled with two black cars. One belonged to my father. The other looked like my Uncle Angelo's.

Crap!

Next came the voices, growing louder with every passing second, and effectively snapping me into action. I refocused my attention on the credenza. Drawers bookended a set of doors about three feet high and four feet wide.

I darted across the room, flung open one of the doors, and climbed inside face forward, curling my body around the reams of paper and boxes of office supplies. The instant the door opened, I shut myself inside, blanketing myself in darkness. My knees poked the underside of my chin, and the corner of a box bit into my hip. The space smelled of dust and oiled hinges.

My heart thudded with reckless abandon, and my blood whooshed through my brain in a crude interpretation of the theme song of *Jaws*. The uneven puffs of my exhalations were deafening in the confined space. I pinched my eyes closed and held my breath, drawing on every survival instinct to remain calm and motionless.

One chair skidded across the hardwood floor,

then another.

"Do you want a drink?" my father's deep voice boomed through the room, sending a shiver shooting between my shoulder blades.

"No drinks for me in the middle of the day. Helena rides my ass about everything these days. What about you, Sal?" the familiar voice of my Uncle Angelo volleyed back.

"Nah. I'm good. I gotta help my brother later," Salvatore D'Amico answered, his honeyed rumble tiptoeing over my skin like a caress. No one had formally introduced me to him, but I'd eavesdropped on his conversations plenty of times. He was a relatively new soldier working under my uncle. Unlike some of the younger guys, who had big tempers and even bigger egos, Sal, as everyone called him, struck me as someone with a good head on his shoulders.

"You're still helping your ma out?" my father asked.

"Yeah, when I can."

I heard the lid pop off my father's whiskey decanter, followed by the clink of glass knocking against glass.

"Good. Good. So what can I do for you?"

My uncle cleared his throat. "We ran into a little problem with Vito Stringari. He was—"

"He was short this month."

"Yeah, and he still hasn't paid last month."

"Why are you bringing this petty shit to me?"

"Well, you know about his kid…"

I felt a tugging sensation on the bottom of my maxi dress. My hands traced the line of my dress, coming to a halt at the door, and that was when I realized my mistake. Somehow I closed it on the hem.

Oh, crap. This is bad. Really bad.

Every choppy mouthful of air was like sandpaper on my cotton-dry tongue. My heart pumped harder than before. A whirlwind of crazy outcomes danced through my head, each worse the last. I'd escaped my father's notice for years, and explained away little inconsistencies with relative ease, but this…this would be unexplainable. His office was firmly planted in the no-go zone. I could count the number of times he told me not to go in here on five people's hands and toes.

"Give him another month." My father's firm bark broke into the stream of deranged thoughts. "Is that it?"

"For now," my uncle replied.

Chairs scraped across the floor again, and with each shuffled footstep out of the room, my muscles unwound fiber by fiber.

"Are you coming, Sal?" my uncle asked.

"I'll catch up with you in a minute. I need to make a call."

CHAPTER TWO

My body tensed like a bowstring in anticipation of the likely confrontation with Sal. Part of me wanted to leap out of the credenza and scream *surprise!*, like this was nothing more than a silly prank gone wrong, but my common sense kept me pinned inside the stifling cabinet. The tapping and pinging of his phone thundered through my ears, each one lulling me into believing he truly didn't realize I was hiding in the room. Maybe he thought the material sticking out of the door was a random chunk of fabric.

I was dead wrong.

In slow motion, the door of the credenza crept open centimeter by centimeter, finally revealing Salvatore D'Amico. He stood squarely with his chin lowered and his black loafer-clad feet more than shoulder width apart. He stared down at me, capturing me in his gaze like the proverbial deer caught in headlights.

The air thickened, and I knew I needed to say something, anything really, except I couldn't find my words. Until this point in time, I'd only seen this man from afar. Up close, he was devastating. Tall and lean, his runner's build was evident even beneath the lines of his fitted black suit. His skin looked like the heavens had sprinkled it with gold dust. And his eyes...well, they reminded me of a kaleidoscope complete with swirls of cinnamon, honey, and speckles of sage, the right one slightly lighter than the left, or maybe it was a trick of the light.

"What are you doing in here?" Salvatore asked, the upward curl of his lips betraying the serious pitch of his voice.

"Oh, um..." I uncurled my legs and scrambled to my feet, careful not to flash my underwear. "I, um, well, you know."

"No, I don't know."

I rolled my shoulders forward and dropped my chin. "It was stupid. I hid when I heard voices. My dad doesn't like it when I come in here."

"Then why were you in here?"

I scanned the room, searching for a plausible excuse. Any excuse. "Uhh...I was looking for a book."

He rubbed his hand across his jaw, his expression inscrutable. "A book?"

"Yeah," I bobbed my head up and down, "a book. I needed something to read. Ya' know how my father hired someone to homeschool me?" At his uncomprehending look, I continued spewing bullshit. "Anyway, the tutor emailed me a reading assignment and I came in here to look for something. I already had one picked out when I heard you guys in the hall. I panicked and hid. It was stupid. I should've left."

I smiled inwardly at my ability to come up with something that wasn't a complete lie. Right after my mom died, my father pulled me out of school and hired a tutor, one I hadn't seen or heard from since I passed my GED three months ago. Sal didn't need to know about that though.

He strolled over to the bookcase and ran a finger along the spines of ten or so books. Without reading the titles, I knew the books were nothing a seventeen-year-old would read voluntarily: the history of winemaking, the fall of the Roman Empire, military strategy, plants, and so on, all of which supported the tutor assignment angle I had pitched him, at least in my mind.

"Which one were you going to read?"

"Any one of them. I'm a history buff and naturalist like my dad. So yeah, I thought I'd find something to occupy myself for the long weekend." I sounded like a rambling idiot. I knew it, and judging from the growing smirk on his face, Sal knew it too. Even worse, I somehow managed to contradict my lie in the span of thirty seconds. I glanced over my shoulder, making sure my father wasn't anywhere in the vicinity before inching my way to the fluted bookcase.

"I'm particularly interested in this one. I'm fascinated with anything dealing with, uh, this topic." I pulled out a book and handed it to him, our fingers brushing for an instant, yet long enough to send a zinger of awareness up my arm.

"Emilia. That's your name, right?" He studied

the book cover and slanted his head to me. My knees wobbled when I caught a hint of his scent—earthy, woody, with notes of cedar. Did he have to smell good too?

"Yep. That's me. Emilia."

"So birds. That's your thing, huh?"

Birds? What the hell was he talking about? Ever since I watched that stupid Alfred Hitchcock film four or five years ago, I was deathly afraid of the winged creatures. Birds, bugs, bats—all of them creeped me the fuck out. My attention dipped to the book title, and my stomach plummeted. *Merda.*

"Uh huh. I love bird watching. It's my thing. I'm even having a bird themed birthday party next month. You know, birds on my cake, bird figurine party favors, feather boas, plastic pink flamingos, bird nests in…well, everywhere really." I checked the urge to shiver.

He wiped a hand over his mouth, clearly hiding a grin because even I couldn't deny I sounded like a total weirdo. "Tell me how old you're going to be again?"

"Eighteen."

"An almost eighteen-year-old bird lover. Interesting hobby you got there. You must be one of the cool kids."

"Well how old are you?"

"Twenty-one in a couple of months."

"Tsk. Tsk. Only twenty and already living a life of crime. Your mom must be so proud."

The study door opened, and I hitched a breath, preparing for a whole new kind of trouble. I should have gotten the heck out of here a long time ago instead of letting Sal distract me.

"Sal, Angelo is ready to head out." My dad's bushy brows slammed together and his lips curled into his mouth at the sight of me. "What are you doing in here, Emilia? You know this room is off limits."

"Uh…" My mind scrambled for a response.

"Emilia dropped in to invite me to her bird-themed birthday party next month."

"She did?" my dad said, his eyes narrowing fractionally. He knew I hated birds. I had a lot explaining to do.

"Um, yeah. I know Gian and Carmela are coming, but it'd be nice to have other youngish people there."

"All right, then." Sal handed me the bird book. "I don't want to keep Angelo waiting. I'll see you later."

When the door closed behind him, I flinched. Sal's presence had sheltered me from my father's unpredictable temper. Now I was on my own, which didn't bode well for me.

"I better get going. I have to prepare for my piano lessons tomorrow." I shoved the bird book back in its place on the shelf.

"Why were you in my study?"

"I was talking to Sal. He seems nice. What's his story?"

"Don't worry about things that don't affect you."

"What's that supposed to mean?"

He ran his finger along the edge of his desk. "Just keep your head down and don't ask questions about things you don't understand."

I shrugged, tamping down the rage building inside of me. My father did everything in his power to keep me in the dark. Too bad for him, because I had no intention of strolling blindly into anything.

"Whatever."

I took two steps toward the door and my dad called out to me. "A bird theme? Really, Emilia? Is that the best you could come up with?"

I shrugged nonchalantly and my body relaxed, realizing he wasn't going to press the issue. "It's about time I got over my fear of birds, don't you think? Besides, Sal seems nice. I like him."

"If you say so."

CHAPTER THREE

In the past month, I'd seen Sal twice in passing since the incident in my father's study. We exchanged simple greetings and a little bit of witty banter, nothing of importance or meaning, though. Given I didn't have a legitimate reason to talk to him, I had no reason to expect anything else. That didn't get in the way of the annoying habit I developed recently that consisted of reliving every shared look and touch and twisting it into something significant. Not that anyone could fault me. A cloistered nun had more freedom than me, so Sal popping in and out of my life was akin to offering a glass of water to someone dying of thirst.

The biggest question lingering was why Sal had covered for me. Granted, he didn't outright lie to my dad. I considered it more of an omission. My father wouldn't care about the semantics, and Sal would be in deep shit if my dad discovered he hadn't been entirely forthright.

My dad turned on some music and faint notes of Frank Sinatra floated through the air. You'd think he would play something more age appropriate for my birthday, but no, not my father. Everything revolved around him and what he liked. I glared at the clock on my phone, willing the minutes to pass. I couldn't stop thinking about whether Sal would make an appearance.

God, I wanted him to. He'd become my dirty little obsession. Rather than practice for my upcoming recital, I daydreamed about Sal showing up, whisking me off to some secluded location and confessing he liked me and wanted to spend time with me. This wouldn't be out of the ordinary for most eighteen-year-olds, except I wasn't like the rest of the girls my age.

As a general rule, I never put much stock into what people thought of me. I didn't care about making friends. I never had a crush on anyone, male or female. I only cared about escaping the arranged marriage looming in my future like a date with the guillotine…until now, and it scared me.

"Ugh." I jammed the heel of my hand into my forehead.

I needed to pull my head out of my ass. Ten minutes until my birthday party officially started, and instead of thinking about celebrating turning into an adult, I was behaving like a lovesick preteen.

I couldn't afford to get sidetracked with a stupid crush that could never go anywhere. I owed it to my mom to break my father's hold on me. She wanted the two of us to start a new life away from him, and I fully intended to fulfill her dying wish.

My cousins Gian and Carmela barged into the

house laughing and joking with each other, and I rolled my eyes. Truthfully, I'd always been a little jealous of them. They had a mother, a father, and each other. I had nobody, not since my mom died anyway. My dad acted like a jail warden, not a parent.

"Happy birthday to my favorite dark fairy," Gian said, ruffling his hand through my hair before drawing me into a tight hug.

As much as there was a wedge of age and awkwardness between my extended family and me, they never failed to treat me kindly. They hugged and kissed me all the time, which wasn't surprising. The Trassatos were a family of huggers and kissers, showering everyone with love and affection. My father and I were the anomalies, cold to their warmth, dark to their light. I never could figure out what made us different. Maybe it was because my mom wasn't one of them and never wanted to be. Or maybe because her death had emotionally handicapped both of us.

"Screw you, *Gianluca*." I drew out his full name, knowing he disliked it as much as I hated the little nickname he and his sister gave me. So what? I liked the color black. A lot. It fit my mood.

"Pleasant as ever, I see."

"Gian, be nice. It's her birthday. You know she doesn't like that nickname," Carmela chastised, shoving her long wavy hair over her shoulder and pressing a kiss to each of my cheeks. She'd been dating Rocco for as long as I could remember, and she was beautiful in a sexy way that drove guys crazy. In a nutshell, she was my polar opposite.

When people looked past my all black clothing, they called me cute, adorable, and tiny.

Gian grinned. "Jesus, lighten up. I was kidding."

"Yeah. Whatever." I raked my middle finger up the side of my face, my smile growing with every centimeter.

Scanning the decorations, his meaty paw came down on my shoulder, and he shivered mockingly. "Holy shit. What happened in here? Did somebody kill Big Bird?"

I cringed. Feathers were scattered on top of the tables like confetti. A spun sugar bird nest filled with brightly colored candy eggs perched on top of the cake. Fake birds hung from the light fixtures, taunting me with their beaks and beady eyes. It was like my personal nightmare had come to life.

"What can I say? I love birds."

"Uh huh." Gian popped open the bottle of Limoncello tucked under his arm and filled three plastic glasses with the greenish-yellow syrupy spirit. I loved Limoncello, and luckily for me, he brought the good stuff.

I wasn't old enough to drink, but our family didn't care about legalities. I could have a drink on occasion as long as I didn't abuse the privilege or embarrass my family. My father waxed poetic on more than one occasion about the wisdom of his parents serving him watered down wine with dinner from the time he turned eight. He firmly believed that introducing alcohol in small doses at a younger age reduced the likelihood of overindulging in the future.

Carmela handed Gian and me a glass and raised

hers in the air. "Happy Birthday, Emilia, our favorite cousin."

I tapped both of their glasses and gulped down the fiery sweet liquid. "Another," I croaked.

Humor shining in his golden eyes, Gian filled my glass again, and I immediately tossed back the contents. I needed it if I wanted to get through this party without either constantly searching for Sal or being reduced to tears by the freakish feathered creature display.

Three and a half shots later—Gian ripped the last one away from my mouth before I could finish it—I roamed the party with a smirk on my face and feeling lighter than I had in years.

People patted me on the head asked me questions about my piano lessons and what I'd been up to in the past month or two. I offered a bunch of meaningless responses because my only plan was escaping this life, and I could only imagine the look on their faces if I blurted out the truth.

When nine o'clock rolled around and Sal still hadn't made an appearance, I slipped out the back door and curled up beneath my favorite tree. I had tea parties with imaginary friends in this same spot, climbed the tree to study the stars, took shelter in the branches when I didn't want to hear my parents fighting, and grieved beneath it when my mom died. It was the one place where my days didn't feel so heavy.

Staring back at the yellow lights of the home I shared with my dad, the brisk spring air pebbling my skin, I finally let the disappointment come. I couldn't explain why I cared Sal hadn't bothered to show his face tonight. He hadn't given me any indication he wanted to be friends or anything else for that matter.

CHAPTER FOUR

"Hey, what's the birthday girl doing out here?"

My stomach flipped at the sound of Sal's voice. I glanced up and caught him striding across the yellowed grass without a care in the world. He crouched down in front of me, a box wrapped in brown paper with a pink feather boa knotted around it dangling from one hand. Too busy looking him up and down because I could scarcely believe he was real, I didn't say a word for a long beat. Sal was *here* at *my* house for *my* birthday party. Holy crap. He actually came.

"Just getting some air," I finally answered.

"You look sad. Are you going to tell me what's goin' on? Did someone upset you?"

His question hung in the air, and without evaluating the consequences, I blurted out the truth. "I didn't think you were coming."

He rubbed his hand along his jaw. "Yeah, sorry about that. I had some stuff to take care of. It took longer than I expected, but I come bearing gifts."

He held up the box, rattled it, and set it down

next to me.

"Thank you."

"Come on." He tapped the top of the box with a finger. "Open it up. I want to know if you like it."

"Right now?"

"No, next week." He smirked, his brownish green eyes dancing with far too much amusement. "What do ya think?"

"Jerk," I mumbled, tearing the pink boa off the package and draping it around my neck despite my total hatred of everything feathered. I ripped into the wrapping paper and opened the box. "Binoculars?"

"Yup. I figured you could do all the spying or bird watching you wanted without straining your eyes."

I nodded, pulling out the binoculars. "Wow. Thanks."

I held them to my eyes, pretending to test them out even though I couldn't see a damn thing in the dark. Truthfully, I was doing my best to disguise the rush of too revealing emotions surely carved into my face. Until I opened Sal's present, I didn't realize how much I missed actually receiving a gift someone put thought into.

My family had given up trying to buy me anything years ago when they figured out I religiously returned all their gifts for money if possible. While I appreciated their efforts, I was more concerned with padding my escape fund. After two years, they all caught on and started stuffing some cash in an envelope, saving all of us the hassle.

"You like 'em?"

"Yeah." My voice splintered, and I pulled them away from my face. "I really do."

Sal pushed my hair behind my ears and tipped my face toward the inky sky with two roughened fingers. "You have the most beautiful neck I've ever seen. You should wear your hair tied back like this more often. You remind me of a ballerina, all dainty and fine boned."

Awareness flickered across his face, and all I could think was that he wanted to kiss me. Neither of us moved, and I held my breath, silently praying he would do it. He didn't. The tips of his fingers painted a line from the bottom of my ear to the hollow of my neck.

"Thanks," I whispered, hedging toward him until I could see every golden and mossy green fleck in his eyes.

He cleared his throat and his hand dropped to my lap, his fingers playing with mine. "Did you get everything you wanted?"

I debated my answer for a split second and lifted my chin. "No. Not yet, but I'm hoping there are still some surprises in store for me. Maybe you can help me. I *am* the birthday girl after all. I'm pretty sure you have a duty to make all my wishes come true."

"Hmm. Is that right?"

"Would I lie to you?"

One side of his mouth hooked up and I swear on everything holy my stomach fluttered. "That's up for debate, but I'll play along for now. What do you want?"

"So, um, I'm eighteen now and all, and I-I…"

My courage stalled and I couldn't get the request out of my mouth. I rolled my neck in a circle, unscrambling the tangled thoughts clouding my brain. He could say no, and without a doubt, I'd feel uncomfortable every time we ran into each other, and that was all right. I didn't plan to remain under my father's roof for more than another year anyway.

"I want a birthday kiss," I blurted before my pride had the chance to edit my request.

His hand abandoned mine. "You do?"

"From you," I added, heat crawling up my neck. *Thank God for the darkness.*

He glanced at the house and rubbed the back of his neck. "That's not gonna happen."

"Why?"

"Well, for starters, I think your dad would put a bullet between my eyes."

"My dad is holed up in the study with the rest of the men drinking bourbon and smoking cigars."

"That explains why it looked like a girls only party inside."

"Yep."

The corners of his eyes crinkled, taking me in and clearly deliberating the pros and cons of my request.

"In that case…" He tugged on my sleeve, pulling me closer to him. "I think I need to do my duty and grant the birthday girl her wish."

"You do," I rasped out, my eyelids heavy, my heart racing, and my lips tingling in anticipation.

Not a second later, his lips were on mine and a quick gasp flew out of my lungs, searing a path right past my parted lips. The kiss was so gentle I questioned whether I imagined it. He lingered there, not taking it any further. When he started to lean back, I whimpered, desperate for him to keep going and do something forbidden.

"Not enough?" His voice sounded gravelly and his eyes darkened.

My fingers dug into the tight weave of his dark shirt, my breaths choppy.

"Noted," he whispered, his lips slanting against mine. They were warm and smooth and tasted smoky with a hint of honey. Every brush sent chills down my spine and doubled my heartbeat.

His tongue swiped across the seam of my lips before working its way inside my mouth. I moaned, and it was like throwing gasoline on fire. His arms circled my body and my back collided with the roughened bark of the tree. His hands moved up and down my sides, and my fingers speared into his thick waves. I transferred every emotion inside of me into that kiss: happiness, awe, loneliness, and a touch of anger and helplessness.

Sal's hips wedged between mine, his mouth traveling to the pulse points next to my ear and at the hollow of my neck. His hands snuck under the hem of my dress and my leg muscles contracted beneath his fingers. Even in my lust-intoxicated state, I knew this didn't resemble a sweet birthday kiss. I needed to pull the plug on this half-baked idea before my father got a wild hair up his ass and came outside looking for me. Only I couldn't.

And like some divine creature heard my warring sentiments, Sal's phone rang. He pulled back, chilly air quickly replacing the sizzling warmth of his body. With his heavy eyelids and his bee-stung mouth, he certainly lived up to all the stupid daydreams that had monopolized my brain over the past month. I still couldn't believe he actually came to my birthday party out of all of the places he could be on a Friday night, and he kissed me out of all of the women he knows.

Best birthday present ever.

"I'm sorry." He raked his teeth over his lower lip. "I didn't mean for it to go that far."

His apology hit my chest with the force of a punch. I'd rather he said nothing than apologize. Outside of Gian and Carmela, everyone treated me with kid gloves, and I suspected it had to do with who my father was more than anything else.

"No worries. It was the perfect first kiss." He frowned, and I rushed to alleviate his fears. "There's no reason to freak out. I won't tell anyone." I made an invisible x over my heart. "I promise."

He glanced over his shoulder, studying my house. "I need to get back to work. I only had a quick break, but I wanted to give you that present and say happy birthday."

"Oh, okay. So when will I see you again?"

"Soon, I'm sure." He pressed a kiss to my forehead and climbed to his feet. "*Ciao, tesoro. Vivere una vita bella.*"

"Bye, Sal." He vanished around the side of the house to the front yard, his dark clothing and hair blending like a specter into the starless sky.

CHAPTER FIVE

I slinked inside the kitchen door of my house, hoping to avoid any witnesses and bolt up the service stairs to my bedroom. I slammed the back door shut behind me, and pressed one of my hands to my still tingling lips. I held back a giggle. I couldn't believe he kissed me, like *really* kissed me. Other than his apology at the end, the moment couldn't have been more mind-blowing.

"You like him, don't you?"

My arm dropped to my side. Letizia DiMartino stood in front of the white farm sink, staring out the window. Most people called her Lettie. She'd married one of my dad's capos, Pietro, five years ago. I went to the wedding, and I remembered thinking she looked so somber even when she smiled.

After cutting the cake, I found her crying in the bathroom, and she confessed that she didn't want to marry Pietro. When I asked her why she did it, she shrugged and said she didn't have a choice. I told her I'd run away before I married an old man. She said I was braver than her. For some reason, that moment stuck in my psyche as an omen of what would happen if I didn't escape this life before my father succeeded in marrying me off to some stranger.

Over the years she always made a point to talk to me. She was ten years older than me, so we were in completely different places in our lives, albeit that didn't prevent us from becoming unlikely confidants. We bonded over our shared misery. She desperately wanted out of her marriage, and I wanted to make a new life in another place where I didn't have to worry about being a Trassato. While I wouldn't call us best friends, my father gave me some freedom to hang around her because of her connection to Pietro and the Family.

"Who?"

A sly grin came over her face. "Sal. Who else would I be talking about?"

"Oh." I traced the crevice in the herringbone set hardwood with the toe of my black ballet flats. "I didn't realize you knew him."

"Yeah. You didn't know he lived with us a while back?"

"No. You never said anything."

She shrugged. "It wasn't a big deal. Pietro moved Sal's family into our guesthouse after his dad died. I think he wanted to make sure they landed on their feet."

"They still live there?"

"No. Once Sal graduated from high school, Angelo took him under his wing, and they moved out shortly after that. I heard Sal rented a little apartment for his mom and brother."

"Oh." My shoulders sunk, and I bit my lower lip. "So you know him well then."

Something resembling jealousy flared in the pit of my stomach. I didn't like the idea of Sal being friends with Lettie. She was older, sophisticated, and in my opinion much prettier than me. Not a piece of her long shiny hair dared to fall out of place. Her makeup invariably hit the right note between not enough and way too much. She had one of those smiles that lit up a room. *Ugh.* I didn't want to think about it.

"Somewhat. Although I don't think anyone knows Sal all that well. We hung out on occasion, but he spent most of the time doing whatever it took to get into Pietro's good graces."

"Yeah, um, I guess that makes sense."

"So what's going on between you two?"

"Nothing really. He had a meeting with my father, and we talked in passing. We've run into each other a couple of times since then, and he's nice. You could say we're friends."

"It looked like more than that to me."

That comment answered the question lingering in my mind about whether she had seen us kissing. Flames rolled up my face, and I caught her eye before quickly looking away. As much as I wanted to trust Lettie, she was kind of a wildcard, and I couldn't risk anything getting back to my father. Without exception, he shut down any interaction with the opposite sex if they weren't related to me.

"Trust me. It wasn't a big deal. I don't expect anything to come out of it. You know how my dad is. He keeps me under lock and key most of the time except for those dumb piano lessons and family social events."

She arched an eyebrow. "If you say so."

"Even if I wanted something to happen between Sal and me, and I don't, it would be impossible. Knowing my dad, he's probably going to force me to marry some connected asshole in Chicago or maybe the Mickey Mouse Mafia in LA if I'm lucky. I'd love to get far away from this place."

I laughed off my statement despite the fact it was so close to the truth, my stomach literally rolled with nausea. While the great Dominick Trassato hadn't come right out and told me of his intentions, I overheard enough to know he had been negotiating my marriage to Master Marcello, whoever the hell that was, since before my mom died. My father could plot and plan until his face turned blue though, because I'd never marry someone beholden to him.

"Yeah. Dominick would rip Sal a new asshole if he found out he touched you, and it's probably for the best. I know Sal seems like a nice guy, but he's got a dark side like the rest of the men associated with this family. And trust me, the dark side always comes out when you least expect it."

My eyes widened, and I grabbed her hand, squeezing it. "Oh crap, Lettie. Did Pietro hit you again?"

I had no clue how often Pietro roughed her up. I'd seen finger-shaped bruises on her upper arms once about a year ago, and a split lip six months before that. She didn't elaborate other than to say she and Pietro had a disagreement.

She blinked rapidly, then pushed her envy-inducing silky hair away from her face. "I don't want to talk about it."

"You need to tell someone. You can't keep living like this."

She covered her face with her hands. "You're right. I know I should do something, but I can't. I don't have a job, I don't have any money, and my family won't help me. My parents think I'm lucky to have him after everything that happened before...you know."

She'd never clarified how she wound up married to Pietro, but I heard plenty of rumors. Apparently, she was dating some guy she went to NYU with, and she got pregnant. He freaked out and forced her to get an abortion. Somehow her parents found out and made her drop all of her classes and marry Pietro.

"We'll figure this out."

"No. No." She dropped her hands to her sides and backpedaled a few steps. "I don't want you to get involved. I'll take care of it. I'm working on something."

"Oh. Okay. That's good."

"Yeah, so anyway, enough of my baggage." She pulled me into a hug, and her spicy cinnamon smell enveloped me. "Happy birthday, Emilia."

"Thanks for coming, Lettie."

"Where else would I be? You're the only thing resembling a friend I have these days. None of the other wives like me."

I stepped out of her embrace and gave her a

halfhearted smile. "Yeah, well, it's their loss." I knew what she meant. The other wives shot her glares when no one was looking. I didn't get it, and I didn't expect to. Without a mother, I wasn't privy to the gossip of the women in the family.

"So what'd Sal get you?"

"Oh." I chuckled sheepishly. "Binoculars."

"Binoculars? What's that about?"

"I guess it's kind of an inside joke."

"Care to elaborate?"

"Not really." I lifted one shoulder. "It's just me being a dork, that's all. Nothing exciting."

"Right, well..." She glanced at her silver wristwatch with diamonds lining the face. As much as she claimed to hate Pietro, he showered her with expensive gifts. Designer clothes, jewelry dripping with precious stones, and expensive purses that would pay most people's rent for a month or two. "I should get home. You know how Pietro is. He'll have a list of accusations to throw in my face if I stay much longer. I'm sorry."

"Don't worry about it. It's not a big deal. I'm going to sneak up to my room now anyway."

She snorted. "That's a good idea. The *wives* have quarantined themselves in the living room to gossip about everyone who isn't here, and the men are doing their thing in the study."

"What about Gian and Carmela? Are they still here?" They were the only people who might notice my absence.

"No. They took off about a half an hour ago."

"Then I've done my duty."

She tugged on the pink boa around my neck. "By

29

the way, I like this look on you. With the black shift dress, your hair pulled back, and the boa, you remind me of a flapper girl. It's cute, but you always look so cute."

I rolled my eyes and pulled her in for another hug. "Yeah, whatever. Being cute is overrated. I wish I looked more like you. I'm pretty sure the wives are all jealous. That's why they act so cold toward you."

"It's a lot more complicated than that. See you later, Emmie."

CHAPTER SIX

I paused mid-descent of the front steps from my piano teacher's brownstone. The balmy spring day air embraced me, reminding me summer was right around the corner. Closing my eyes, I raised my face to the sky, letting the sunshine warm my face.

"Emilia."

I opened my eyes, and my stomach clenched. "What are you doing here?"

Sal pushed away from the iron railing, his arms folded across his navy suit jacket and dark aviator glasses shielding his eyes. "Gian had some stuff to take care of so I volunteered to pick you up."

"Um, yeah, no thanks. I'll pass."

He opened up the back passenger door of a black sedan with dark tinted windows. "Come on. Get in the car. I don't have time to dick around right now."

"Then don't. I'll find my way home."

I skirted around the open car door and trotted the down the sidewalk, my black lace-up boots clipping a panicky metronome over the concrete. Nearly two and a half months had elapsed since he kissed me on my birthday, and every day my anger grew and grew both at him and myself. The five or six times I saw him he looked right through me like I didn't exist. An invisible nobody. Someone completely beneath his notice.

The first encounter felt like he plunged a dagger into my chest. I'd spent the ten days between my birthday and that moment dreaming up all these scenarios where we'd start dating, he'd profess his undying love for me, and we'd live happily ever after.

When I recognized his voice in my father's study, I lingered outside the wood and glass double doors, drinking in the chiseled angles of his face and the way his shoulders filled out his suit. By the time he emerged from the room, my face was heated from waxing poetic about his masculine beauty. To my horror, he sauntered right by me, offering nothing more than a frown and slight pursing of his lips.

I still didn't give up hope. Nope, I rationalized his behavior a million different ways all of which fed my unhealthy infatuation. After five more weeks and a handful of meetings where he couldn't be bothered to mumble a greeting, I got his message loud and clear. He didn't want anything to do with me, and I had experienced enough rejection in my life without willingly inviting more.

The chance run-in outside the office of my father's bar completed my trifecta of humiliation. He had his arm around some blonde woman who was my complete antithesis. Curvy to my petite frame, colorful dress to my drab black t-shirt and boyfriend jeans, light to my dark, sexy to my cute, carefree to my moodiness.

And like magic, the final remnants of my obsession with him died a hard, cold death. Summoning my best poker face, I looked right through him like I didn't know who he was. Like he never meant anything to me. I'd worked hard to keep him from intruding in my thoughts since then, which underscored why I needed to get the hell away from him before I relapsed like the Sal junkie I was. While I could delude myself with the best of them, the way my heart leaped and my nerve endings tingled when I heard his voice told me all I needed to know. Despite all my efforts, my fascination with him was alive and well.

"Godammit," he grumbled from behind me, the car door slamming with a loud *thud*. "I don't have time for this shit."

"Good, then we're on the same page. Do what you need to do and leave me alone."

His hand clamped like a vise on my shoulder, and he spun me around. "The fuck, Emilia?"

"Don't touch me!"

He raised his hands in the air next to his head. "What's wrong with you?"

"Why are you here?"

"I told you already. Gian needed—"

"No. The real reason. Gian could've called Carmela, my Aunt Helena, anybody really. You'd be the absolute last person he'd send to pick me up, which means you offered. I know that doesn't make any sense considering how cold you've been since my birthday. That's the only reason I can think of."

He ripped his sunglasses from his face and hung them from the collar of his shirt. He tipped his head to the brilliant blue sky, his hands buried deep in his pockets. I drank in the clean lines of his face and exaggerated pout of his lower lip like I was dying.

Evidently, his physical and mental distance made it easy to forget how attractive he was, which made it even more imperative to get the hell away from him. Nothing and no one could convince me to risk a thirty-minute drive home in close quarters with him where I'd further commit his smell and the unique color of his eyes to memory.

"Look, Em, I—"

"Emilia," I growled, hating how much I liked the nickname on his lips.

"Fine. Emilia. Is that better?" I nodded, and he blew out a breath. "Kissing you was a mistake. You're eighteen, and I'm twenty-one. If your dad found out I took advantage of you, he would fit me with a pair of cement boots."

I ground my teeth together until I could suppress my hurt and anger enough to reply. "I agree. It was a mistake."

"You agree?" He sounded confused, as if he couldn't believe I would have given up on him so easily.

Well, he underestimated me, because I would rather stomp on a bed of hot coals than beg for scraps of attention or affection from him or anyone else. It was one of the few lessons my father taught me that I took to heart. Love not given freely wasn't worth my time. I wholeheartedly agreed.

"Yep, especially since you seemed to read a lot

34

more into it than I did. What'd you think? One kiss and I'd demand a marriage proposal?"

"Well, you fooled me because you seemed pretty into me that night."

With hooded eyes, his gaze slowly dragged up and down my body, and some mixture of a shiver and a thrill arrowed through me. Well, that settled it. I couldn't trust myself not to do something stupid like ask him to kiss me again, or worse, plead with him for a morsel of affection.

I ripped my phone from my pocket and summoned the closest car. Lucky for me, one was less than a minute away.

"I must be a good actress because I haven't thought about the kiss or you since that night."

"Is that a fact?" He inched closer to me until the tips of his black loafers brushed against the toes of my boots.

"Yes." My voice wavered, and I wanted to slap myself across the face.

"Now you've got me curious."

His body pitched toward me, and I smelled his minty breath. I saw each sooty blade of his lashes and the forest green rim around his otherwise golden brown eyes. My knees wobbled, and the corners of his mouth twitched, drawing my gaze to that cute dent in the center of his lower lip.

"Oh, yeah? What about?"

"Your lips."

"My lips?" I parroted. My voice sounded rusty, and I clamped my mouth shut with the sole goal of circumventing my traitorous body's urge to betray me more than it already had.

He glanced at my lips. "I remember them being so soft."

My heart nearly flew out of my chest, and I couldn't think of a single think to say in response. He shifted, his lips only a centimeter from mine, maybe less. Giddy with anticipation, my blood hummed, and all of my self-righteous rage evaporated like a tendril of smoke. There I stood like a lamb being led to slaughter, my eyes fluttering and my chin lifted invitingly.

Do it.

Sal pulled back. "That's what I thought." He enunciated each word like a master of ceremonies announcing the winner of a boxing match. Maybe he was, and I definitely came out as the loser.

My eyes popped open, and I blinked. Humiliation rushed fast and hard through my veins, multiplying my barely suppressed anger tenfold. A choking sound erupted from my mouth, and I felt sick deep down in the pit of my stomach. The fact that any two-timing molecule of my body craved a kiss from him pissed me off. I was full-on stupid. There was no other explanation.

"Now get in the car, and I'll take you home. As fun as this has been, I don't have any more time to play games with you."

Not a second too soon the car I summoned pulled to the curb and the driver rolled down the window. "Emilia?"

"Todd?" I said, recalling the name of the driver from the app on my phone.

"That's me."

I glanced at Sal as I climbed in the car. "Well,

I'll hopefully see you again, um, never." Smirking, I slammed the door closed. Sal took a step forward, his eyebrows plaited together and his lips curled over his teeth. Oh shit, he was mad.

"Can we go please? This guy is harassing me," I said, my voice breathy and rushed.

"You got it."

A chorus of honks and crude hand gestures accompanied the driver's sharp swerve into oncoming traffic. I slumped down in my seat and covered my face with my hands.

What the hell was that about?

CHAPTER SEVEN

"I can't believe your dad actually let you out of the house."

I set my cappuccino on the round table and pulled out a metal chair across from Lettie. "He lets me go places."

"Oh please. You can't even take a stroll around the block without a guard. He must really want you to learn how to play the piano if he's allowing you out of the family compound twice a week."

I glanced nervously at the door. Tony, or Tony Red as everyone called him, sat at an empty table with his back to the wall. Lately, he'd become my official babysitter. I guess Gian was too busy to be bothered with me now that he was officially a made man. Apparently, they were grooming Gian for bigger and better things, whereas Tony didn't have the aptitude to be anything other than a soldier. While he made a decent enforcer, he didn't have much earning potential. I could see their point. He gave the impression of being short on independent thought and dimmer than a burnt out light bulb.

I hitched my thumb over my shoulder in Tony's general direction. "Well, you're right about that. I definitely have a babysitter today. That's the only reason I'm here."

Lettie leaned forward conspiratorially, lowering her voice a notch and hiding one side of her mouth with a perfectly manicured hand. "Too bad, your dad didn't pick Sal. That would've been much more entertaining. Tony is such a dud."

Bitterness bubbled up my throat at her reference to Sal. I hadn't seen him since he toyed with me after my piano lesson, which was all right with me. I'd be perfectly content to avoid him for the rest of my life. It still irked me that he had to get in that last dig instead of allowing me to walk away with my dignity intact.

"Tony's not so bad," I answered, not wasting any brainpower on Sal. As far as I knew, no one except Lettie witnessed our kiss during my birthday party, and I wanted to keep it that way. Eventually, the whole debacle would be relegated to the dustbin of irrelevant events.

"Maybe you're right. I don't know Tony that well. He works with your uncle most of the time, not Pietro." She took a sip of her coffee, her eyes glued to me. "So what's the deal with you and Sal? You haven't mentioned him since your birthday, and I gotta admit I'm kind of surprised. You looked all excited when you came inside after sucking face with him."

Cringing, I glanced over my shoulder making sure Tony wasn't listening to our conversation. I didn't want word to get back to my dad. He'd have ten people following me around if he got a whiff of anything remotely improper happening between Sal and me. Even worse, he'd punish Sal, and although I considered him a giant asshole, I didn't want to sic my dad on him. Luckily, Tony was absorbed in a phone conversation.

"I already told you, the thing with Sal wasn't a big deal. He kissed me. We haven't talked much since, and I don't expect anything to happen between us. I want to make a break from the family, and he's busy building a life as one of my dad's minions. End of story."

"I know, but you wouldn't be the first girl to get sidetracked by a pretty face, and Sal has one helluva face."

"Eh, he's okay," I lied, internally lamenting that God wasted such good looks on a conceited prick like Sal.

"Oh shut up." She shoved me in the arm. "You can't deny he's one fine specimen even if you don't like him. If I weren't married to Pietro the Warden I'd be interested."

"Don't call your husband that. Tony might hear you. Then they'll know you know."

"I don't care. The guys call him that, why can't I? After all, it's true. He kept that man chained up in our basement and—"

I slapped my hand over her mouth. "Stop talking about that. You know nothing good will come of bringing that up. You'll be considered an accessory because you didn't do anything about it."

She dragged my hand from her mouth. "I didn't have a choice, obviously, and I wasn't supposed to know about it. I never would've if I didn't stumble onto that surveillance video." She raised her eyebrows. "And don't forget, you're the one who suggested I snoop around the house, so I hold you partially responsible."

"I was joking. I didn't think you'd actually do it." I leaned forward. "By the way, did you keep a copy of it?"

"Fuck no. I didn't want anything like that in my possession. It'd be like signing my death warrant. Besides, those videos automatically delete every twenty-four hours."

"Did you ever find out who he was?"

She trailed her finger along the rim of the white coffee mug, her eyes downcast. "No. I didn't even try. More than likely he was some shmuck who owed Pietro money. A nobody who gambled away his family's future."

"Probably. You can't be right in the head if you go to Pietro or my dad looking for a loan."

"That or you're incredibly desperate."

Uncomfortable with the turn of our conversation, a lump threatened to clog up my throat. I agreed to meet Lettie to take my mind off all the bad shit in my life. Yet, somehow my dad's extracurricular activities always managed to irrevocably shape every facet of my life. Permanently severing ties to the Trassatos was the only way to get out from under his shadow.

"How's Alessandro?"

Lettie leaned back in her chair as if she were contemplating solutions to solving world hunger. Alessandro was Pietro's son. I didn't know much about his mother. Nobody talked about her, which was understandable. Apparently, she turned up pregnant when they were both eighteen. She didn't want anything to do with Pietro's world or raising a kid, so she left Alessandro with Pietro and took off.

"He's in college. NYU or something, so I hardly see him, which is fine with me." Her lips puckered. "He's a spoiled prick who thinks he's too good for everyone, and Pietro feeds into the whole delusion by pretending the world revolves around his prodigal son."

Lettie made no secret of the fact she didn't like Alessandro, and he didn't hide that the feelings were mutual. When I pried into what happened between them, she shrugged it off and called him a brat. I liked him, though. He was funny and honest, both things in short supply in my life.

"Does Pietro still want to have more kids?"

She forced out an exaggerated shiver punctuated with a snicker. "I'm not that stupid. I don't want anything tying me to him for life, so I've taken precautions to ensure it's impossible."

Tony tapped me on the shoulder. "It's time to go, Miss Trassato. Your lesson starts in ten minutes."

I sighed, and Lettie smirked.

"You better get going, Em." She winked. "I know how much you want to be a concert pianist when you grow up."

Like so many things in my life, I wasn't entirely sure playing piano was my dream and not my dad's. I couldn't remember a time when he hadn't dictated my choices, and for too many years I willingly went along for the ride.

He had some delusion that he could mold me into a new and improved version of my mom, the great Ava Accorso. She was a notable Italian-born concert pianist. Prior to meeting my dad, she had performed all over the world as a soloist, recitalist, and chamber musician. She even won numerous international competitions.

In fact, that's how they met. She was performing at some private party where my dad was a guest. Smitten with her, he waited outside until she left and offered her a ride home. Despite the protests of her family, they dated for two short months before they were married, and I came around nine months later. The rest is history.

"You know me so well, Lettie," I retorted, my voice chock full of sarcasm.

She snorted. "That I do. Have fun banging on the piano. Hopefully it will help you work out your bad mood. Oh, and let me know if anything happens with you know who."

I glared at her, telling her with the invisible flames shooting out of my eyes to shut the fuck up. "You'll be the first to know if my dad agrees to let me be part of the Christmas performance," I shot back, seamlessly blurting out a lie to cover her statement.

I gathered my cappuccino and followed Tony out the door. I didn't have a clue why Lettie was so up my ass about Sal. I wished she'd shut the hell up. Her loose lips were a potent reminder of all the reasons why I needed to quit confiding in her. While we were friends of sorts, Lettie liked to joke about the things I told her. She swore it kept the crappy parts of our lives bearable. I didn't always agree, particularly when it could easily upend my plans. I couldn't afford to take that chance or I'd find myself married off to Marcello.

CHAPTER EIGHT

After my piano lesson, I climbed into the passenger seat of Tony's black sedan, digging around in my purse for my phone.

"Tony," I said without looking up, "my dad won't be home for dinner so I want to swing by that deli on 54th on the way home to grab something to eat. I'm starving."

"I'm not Tony. Sorry to disappoint." Sal turned to face me from the driver's seat, a huge grin splitting the lower half of his face.

I lunged for the door handle, desperate to get out of the car. The thirty-minute drive in his company would be like a life sentence. The instant my hand closed around the handle, he pulled away from the curb and into the steady stream of traffic.

"Pull over and let me out."

"No can do."

I sunk my fingers into the oyster-colored leather seats. "Where is Tony?"

"Your Uncle Angelo needed him to do some stuff this afternoon."

"What about Gian?"

"He's busy too."

"Lucky me," I responded, my voice utterly and hopelessly flat.

"So what's this place on 54th?"

"Don't worry about it. I'll find something to eat when I get home."

He frowned. "Are you sure?"

"Yep."

"In that case, do you mind running a quick errand with me?"

Do I mind?

Of course, I minded. I preferred to spend as little time as possible in his company. Being around him made me uncomfortable in my skin. He was a shameful reminder that I actually asked, no *begged*, him to kiss me on my birthday. Then, like the dumb little girl wholly lacking in experience with men, I concocted some freakin' fairytale with him in a starring role as Prince Charming.

Ugh.

"I'm kind of tired so I'd appreciate it if you dropped me off first."

"Come on, Emilia." He sighed wearily. "It won't take long. You don't even have to get out of the car. In fact, it'd be better if you didn't."

My head snapped up, way more interested in this errand than two seconds earlier. I needed dirt on my dad's dealings if I wanted to get away from him, and maybe Sal was handing me something on a silver platter.

"What kind of errand?"

A deep chuckle spilled from his lips. "Knowing

your penchant for spying, I should've started there."

"What's this errand?" I asked, ignoring his statement. There was no use denying it. He caught me hiding in my dad's study.

"Just a little something for Pietro."

"Wait…" I leaned forward, bracing my hands on the dash as he whipped around a corner. "I thought you worked with my Uncle Angelo, not Pietro."

He parallel parked in a spot in front of an industrial building with a brick façade and four oversized gray garage doors. Black, red, and blue graffiti marred its smooth concrete sides. It looked like someone had boarded up the windows about a decade ago. The plywood was swollen and splintering around the edges. Yellowed weeds poked holes in the crumbling sidewalk. I'd bet a lot of money the building was crawling with rats and other unsavory creatures. The place should have been condemned. Just looking at it gave me the creeps.

Sal glanced at me as he opened the front driver's door. "What do you know about what I do?"

"Enough." I shrugged. "Like you said, I spend a lot of time gathering information." I had no clue why I confessed that. I needed to practice keeping my thoughts to myself. Sal already proved he wasn't on my side.

"Pietro asked me to pick something up for him. I do him a favor here or there because—"

"Because he took your family in after your dad died."

He rubbed the back of his neck. "Who told you about that?"

"Was it a secret?"

"No."

"Lettie," I answered, watching his face carefully.

He flinched, then smoothed a hand down his face. "Yeah. She mentioned you two were friendly."

"Oh, so you guys kept in touch after you moved out? I didn't realize that."

"What? No. Not even close." His eyes widened. "I stopped by there a couple of days after your birthday and she mentioned your friendship in passing. That's it."

What the hell? Why didn't she bring that up at lunch earlier today?

"Hmm," I murmured. I wanted more details, but I'd wait until I could question her. I didn't like the idea of him thinking I cared about anything he did after he made a joke out of me the last time I ran into him.

He climbed out the car and peered at the vacant building while patting his right side. He was probably double-checking he had a gun. While I'd never attended any so-called business errands with my dad, I'd overheard enough to know anyone with half a brain would never do any mafia business unarmed.

"If I'm not back out in twenty minutes, drive yourself home." He tossed me the car keys and tapped the roof of the car three times. "Got it?"

"Have you lost your mind? I'm not leaving you here."

"Don't worry about me. I can take care of myself."

"Should I call someone to come get you if I take

off?"

"No," he snapped, pinching the bridge of his nose. "Just drive away, leave Tony's car at the end of your block, and forget you ever came here with me."

A current of fear shot down my spine, and if he noticed me shudder, he didn't comment. "I got it. Run away and don't look back."

"Good girl." He flashed me a blatantly false smile and slammed the door. Thirty seconds later he rounded the side of the building with his gun drawn and pointed in front of him, the sunlight glinting off the metal.

CHAPTER NINE

I repeatedly peeked at the clock on the dashboard as I listened to song after song without any of the words or melodies registering in my mind. When thirty minutes passed, my chest tightened with fear and all kinds of theories I refused to verbalize.

Get in the driver's seat and drive home.

I repeated this mantra five or six times, yet my body refused to comply with the order.

"Fuck!" I shouted, the shrillness of my voice echoing in my ears like a taunt. I studied the seemingly vacant warehouse, my heart drumming and my hands trembling. "Goddammit, Sal, why didn't you take me home first?"

I banged my hand against the console. I needed to make a decision either way, because if something bad were going down inside, they'd find me within a matter of minutes, and I didn't know if I could defend myself. The realization made me queasy.

"Screw this," I mumbled, sliding across the front seat and shifting the car into drive. He wanted me to leave and that's precisely what I was going to do. I didn't have to deal with this shit. It was none of my business.

Bang!

A gunshot pierced the silence of the otherwise deserted street. My throat closed on itself, and I blinked back the urge to cry. I fumbled with the latch on the glove box, seeking out the spare gun I knew Tony kept there. When my hand closed around the icy metal grip, I bolted out of the car, not bothering to fully shut the door behind me.

Sprinting around the side of the building, I stuffed the gun into the waistband of my jeans. The hard slapping of my boots against the fractured sidewalk boomed in my ears. My breath came in jagged pants.

Around the back of the building, a man's sprawled out body partially blocked the open metal garage door. Blood dripped from the side of his neck, and his face was locked in a stomach-churning combination of surprise and fear. If I had any sense at all, I would have run when confronted with the sight in front of me.

I stood frozen, my eyes unblinking and my body humming with adrenaline. The scene was like a giant black hole, sucking me into its vortex of terror whether I consented or not.

"Emilia, run! Get the fuck outta here!" Sal's thunderous shout snapped me out of my shock.

I spun on my heel, not making it five feet before I stumbled on the uneven pavement. My knees and hands slammed against the ground, pain vibrating up my limbs. I scrambled forward, crawling like a baby, ignoring the smears of blood on the pavement documenting my pathetic escape attempt.

Someone grabbed me by my hair and jerked me to my feet. My scalp felt like someone had set me on fire. The barrel of a gun pressed against my temple and another arm snaked around my waist.

"Go ahead and try it, Sal," a man behind me growled, his warm expulsion of breath searing the side of my neck.

"Please, no," I mumbled, my legs threatening to buckle under the weight of my mounting hysteria.

Sal stood across from me with his gun raised, his eyes glowing with anger and the muscles in his jaw clenching. "Let her go, Frank."

"Fuck you!" Frank yelled, spittle spraying the side of my neck.

"If you touch her, you're as good as dead. That's Dominick fucking Trassato's only daughter. You harm a hair on her head, and he'll hunt you down and cut you up piece by piece until you're begging for death."

Frank's arm flexed around my waist and his entire body stiffened. "I'm not worried. No one will ever find out I was here today."

"How do you figure?" Sal shot back, closing the distance between us. His gait was graceful and loose-limbed, suggesting he didn't give a shit what happened to me. Maybe he didn't. I was only some random girl he made the mistake of kissing one night. Nothing more.

"I'll kill you both, and Ronny's already dead so I don't have to worry about any witnesses. Sounds clear cut to me."

Sal shrugged, a smug smile sweeping across his

face. "So kill her. I don't give a fuck. She doesn't mean a thing to me, and you'll be playing into my hands. By the time you've wasted a shot on her, I'll have planted a bullet between your eyes. You and Ronny will be dead, and I'll look like a hero, avenging the boss's daughter." His voice was as fluid as molten silver without a single note of hesitation.

I whimpered, my limbs shuddering uncontrollably. Holy shit, this was it. I was going to die, and not only would nobody care, but my dad would probably promote Sal because he wouldn't know any better. Wait, who was I kidding? My dad would probably think *good riddance*. He barely tolerated me these days.

My brain and my emotions disengaged from reality as if I were a bystander watching this from afar. There were only two options right now. I could go on blubbering and pleading for my life, or I could fight. There was a very good chance either option would end with my death, so I decided to fight. I slipped my hand into the waistband of my jeans, shifted the safety on the gun and curled my fingers around the cold, roughcast handgrip, all the while cursing myself for not checking whether the gun was loaded before I embarked on this foolish venture.

Sal and Frank's bickering melded together into fuzzy, indecipherable sounds. My mind zeroed in on the feel of the gun slithering against my flesh and the cold puff of air that brushed across my exposed belly.

Rather than revealing my actions and aiming for

his head or chest, I pointed the gun toward the man's thigh and fired. My ears rang, drowning out the sound of my petrified heartbeat.

"Fucking bitch!" he grunted out, his gun slipping from his hand and spiraling across the ground.

He staggered, taking me with him. My body careened through the air, his arm still around my waist. The second we hit the ground, my skull whipped backward, slamming against his chin. Stars exploded behind my eyes, blurring my vision. Stunned, I froze in place with my back draped over his barrel-shaped chest. The scent of copper filled my nose, and a warm liquid seeped into the back of my jeans.

"Ohmygod, ohmygod," I repeated over and over despite the fact that moving my mouth made me nauseous.

I rolled off him, pulling my knees into my chest. Sal's black tasseled shoes clipped over the concrete, and he kicked the man's gun away. Their bodies collided, pounding each other with bone splitting punches. Sweat and blood flew through the air like a boxing match.

Finally the man fell to his knees and Sal grabbed him by his collar, dragging him inside the building. Within seconds, he had the man's hands and feet bound in a maze of zip ties. I clambered to my feet and headed toward the car.

Sal waved his gun at me. "Hey, Em, whattaya think you're doin'? Get your ass back here."

"No." I swung my head from side to side, the motion making me even dizzier than I already was. "I don't want anything to do with this. I'm gonna get in the car and drive it home. You can find your own way outta here."

"Oh, yeah? You don't want to get mixed up in the family business now that you've seen it firsthand? Well too fucking bad. You should've driven away after twenty minutes like I told you. Now c'mere before someone gets a hair up their ass and comes to investigate."

I wobbled into the warehouse, my knees like jelly and my breathing erratic. The second I stepped foot inside, he pulled the metal garage door shut, the ungreased sound of metal scraping against metal making me jump.

Unruffled, Sal whipped out his phone.

"Tony," he clipped out, "I need a spring cleaner." He paused for a second, listening. "Not an hour from now. I need back up right fucking now. It was an ambush." His gaze met mine and he wiped the blood from his face with the sleeve of his suit jacket. "She's here. Yeah, I know. It's piss poor timing, but I've got it under control." He disconnected the phone and stuffed it in his pocket.

"Who sent you here, Frank?" Sal aimed the gun at his head, enunciating each word with a stony cool that sent a chill down my spine.

"Fuck you. I'm not a snitch."

Sal cocked his gun and grinned. He had an unearthly beauty to him, almost like an avenging angel, only not angelic at all.

"What's wrong? You don't want a clean conscience when you meet your maker?"

"What use do I have for a clean conscience? Just get this over with and go back to your ass kissing.

God knows you'll never be anything more than a puppet dancing to the Trassatos' tune, exactly like your father. I can't believe you're willing to die for them, much less Dominick's spoiled brat."

"You don't know shit."

Frank chuckled. "You wanna know what's funny?"

"No. I want you to shut the hell up. Your thoughts don't interest me."

"I gotta know though. Are you dumb as fuck or are you a brilliant schemer like they say?"

"Since you're the one tied up and about to die, I don't need to answer you, do I?"

"Instead of playing this little game of footsie with the Trassatos, you should come over to the dark side with me. Be your own man." He raised his bound hands and pointed at me, then continued talking, his tone agitated. "Kill her and let's get outta here. I'll tell you everything you wanna know about your dad. Isn't that why you're here? Or does it have something to do with Pietro's bitch? He suspects something's up. Heck, I even have dirt on Dominick. The guys from the old world are itching to take him down if he doesn't keep his end of the bargain this time around. Name what you want. It's yours for the asking."

My mind reeled, attempting to cobble together Frank's words into something that made sense. Names. Places. Faces. All of them flew through my mind with lightning speed. My wayward musings came to a standstill the second my gaze cut to Sal. He whipped a black metal cylinder out of the inside of his black suit jacket, screwed it on the end of his gun, and fired. I jerked back with shock and rammed into the wall. Frank's body slumped to the side, inky blood leaking from the center of his forehead, his eyes fixed and unblinking.

"What'd you do that for?"

"I was tired of listening to him."

"But he knew stuff about your dad and Pietro." My high-pitched voice sounded borderline hysterical even to my own ears.

He shrugged. "He was bluffing."

I blinked rapidly and my vision turned muddy. "You don't know—"

Tony rolled up the metal garage, the rusty metal like nails on a chalkboard. He was flanked by two beefy men I didn't recognize carrying black duffle bags.

Sal scrubbed a hand down his face. "Cutting it close, don't you think?"

"I was across town, doing shit. You know that." Tony's gaze cut to me. "You all right, Miss Trassato?"

I nodded, and the motion caused my entire body to sway like a rag doll. My fingernails scraped on the wall, attempting to catch my balance.

Oh shit.

I didn't feel so good. Sal was across the room lifting me up in a matter of seconds and cradling me in his arms. I burrowed my face into his chest, drinking in his unique smell, now tainted with the metallic scent of death and destruction. Somehow it still managed to be the antidote to everything swirling inside of me.

"She's in shock. I need to get her out of here."

Sal's deep voice vibrated through my limp body, and I didn't think I could open my eyes even if I wanted to. He rubbed my scalp, and I tightened my arms around his neck.

"Yeah. Yeah, get her home."

"Did you reach out to Dominick?"

"Nah, he's got that thing goin' on, and he's out of commission until tomorrow morning."

"I'll get in touch with Angelo, and he can handle Dominick."

CHAPTER TEN

I woke up in my bedroom an unknown number of hours later, not remembering how I got there or who put me there. I rolled onto my back and rubbed my eyes. My body ached, and my head throbbed like someone had hit me with a hammer repeatedly.

"Are you hungry?"

Startled, I shot up in my bed. "Oh, it's you."

Sal had pulled my desk chair up to the side of my bed. His legs were stretched out with his feet resting on the end of the mattress. His hair stuck out in every direction, and more than a days' worth of stubble coated his bronzed face.

I smiled for a second, then everything came back to me and I curled my fingers into my white sheets.

"You were going to let him kill me," I choked out, closing my eyes and turning away from him. He kissed me on a lark, but didn't give a shit if I died, showing me how little he cared. "Get out of my room. Go home. I don't need you here. I'm fine."

He shifted his legs off my bed and rested his

elbows on his knees. "I'll leave when Mr. Trassato returns."

"Ugh." I tossed a pillow at his face, and he batted it away effortlessly. "Go *away*. I don't need a babysitter. My dad leaves me here alone all the time. He knows no one would dare come near his house, much less break in."

"I know."

I scooted away from him, pulled the sheets over my body, and took a deep breath. "Please leave, Sal. I want to be alone. I don't need anything. I promise."

He held up a white paper bag. "Eat first, and then we can talk about whether I'm leaving."

My stomach grumbled. "Is that what I think it is?"

"Yeah." He opened the bag, handed me a lukewarm calzone wrapped in paper, and kept one for himself. "Tony dropped us off some dinner about a half hour ago."

I opened the paper packaging on my lap. The smell of cheese, sausage, warm bread, and roasted red peppers filled the air. I loved this restaurant. It reminded me of my mom's cooking, one more item on a long list of things I missed over the last five years. When she died, she took everything worthy and admirable about our life and family with her.

My dad never laughed anymore. We never had a home cooked meal except on the rare occasion our housekeeper took mercy on us and prepared something, and we didn't talk to each other unless it was absolutely necessary. My dad moved her piano to a guest bedroom so he didn't have to hear me play. As a matter of fact, I had no clue why he insisted I continue taking lessons when he hadn't attended a single one of my performances since her death.

"How long have I been sleeping?"

He crumpled up his wrapper and stuffed it back in the empty bag. "Not long. Maybe two hours."

"Hmm." I finished off the last few bites of my food and tossed the wrapper on the floor. "All right. You got me home and fed me, and I've never been happier. You've done your duty. You can go. I don't need your pity in the form of babysitting *or* kissing."

Mortification burned through me, clamping around my neck like an invisible hand. I swore I had cried my last tear for this man. Being around him made me a person I never wanted to be. My mom cried over my dad too many times, and I promised myself I'd never be the woman who wallowed in her miseries and rejection, yet here I was letting Sal rule my thoughts and emotions.

"*Marone.*" He frowned and clutched the arms of the chair until his knuckles were white. "Pity has nothing to do with me kissing you or staying with you tonight."

"Look," I flipped my hair over my shoulder, "I know you don't want anything to do with me, and I feel the same way. I don't know what possessed me to ask you for a kiss. It was a stupid idea. I got caught up in the celebration. I'm over it now, so there's no need to talk about it."

He climbed into bed and put his arms around me. I wedged my fisted hands between us, creating a physical blockade of sorts, hoping it acted as a mental one too. It didn't work. I melted into him despite my best intentions, feeling safe and warm for the first time since I saw a man die. My spine snapped straight at the memory of men who Sal had shot.

"You killed those two men. What's gonna hap—"

His hand covered my mouth, shutting me down mid-word. I could taste the salt from the calzone on his fingers.

"Shut the hell up," he whispered next to my ear. "You didn't see anything tonight. I drove you home from your piano lesson, and we ate dinner together. That's the official story. Understood?"

I pried his fingers from my face, my eyes wide and my heart thumping like a demon. "Do you think the police are going to come here and—"

"No, Em, they won't. Tony knows what he's doing. Be a good girl and do your part and forget about it. Can you do that?"

When I started to nod, an unwelcome sob burst from my mouth. I swallowed five or more times in a row, battling back the urge to cry, except it wouldn't take no for an answer. My body trembled, tears crawled down my face, and my stomach swirled into knots.

I had spent three years searching for dirt on my dad to get away from him. Now that I had solid proof I didn't want it. I'd give anything to unsee what happened today. The ugly side of the mafia always seemed so far removed from reality when I listened to the whispered conversations and read the cryptic notes. Dead, lifeless eyes brought the horror of this life into sharp focus, and I wanted out more than ever.

"Shh," Sal rocked me from side to side, feathering kisses on my face. "It'll be okay. You're safe. Nothing's going to happen to you. I've got you. I would have died before I let that man hurt you. What I said to him about not caring, that was all for show. It couldn't be further from the truth."

"I don't want to be part of this anymore. I hate what my dad does. I hate him. I hate this life."

"No, you don't. You're in shock right now, and those guys in that warehouse aren't worth crying over. They've killed enough people to fill a bus, so look at it as a good deed. We probably saved dozens of lives today."

I tipped up my chin, studying his solemn face. "You think so?"

"I know so."

"I don't get it. Why were you meeting them?"

"Like I said, Pietro wanted me to do a pick up. It was supposed to be a quick in and out. Grab an envelope and leave. Those men were there, and things went from bad to ugly real fast."

"Do you think someone set you up? Maybe Pietro or Tony?" I should've kept my mouth shut. I knew a little bit about how things worked in my dad's world.

Sal's muscles tensed beneath my fingertips. "Let's not speculate about it, okay? As much as you like to sneak around and spy on your dad, you need to keep your nose out of it. You're gonna hear something you shouldn't, and you'll wind up getting hurt."

"Don't you get it? That's the whole point."

"What the hell are you talking about?"

"I *want* to hear something or know something. It's the only way I'll be able to get away from my father."

The corners of his eyes crinkled, and his lips thinned. "Are you talking about blackmailing your father?"

I swallowed, focusing on gathering my thoughts. The best course of action would be to shut my freakin' mouth. Sal didn't need to know anything about my plans, and history already taught me I couldn't trust him. He had treated me like crap since the night of my birthday party. Something deep inside of me, however, call it gut instinct or whatever, urged me to give him a chance, and that's how I found myself spilling the truth.

"It's my only option. My dad has all these plans for me, and I don't want anything to do with him or his little empire."

"What are you talking about?"

I leaned against the headboard and closed my eyes for a second. "He plans to marry me off to some guy in Chicago to expand his influence. Master—"

"Master Marcello," Sal nodded. "Otherwise known as Marcello Masciantonio."

"Yeah, that's him. I've overheard my dad negotiating with some men more than a few times in the last six months. I don't want to be married to some guy in another state I don't know."

Sal shifted onto the bed, his legs dangling off the

edge, and his back facing me. "Hmm. I don't know anything about that."

"Do you know Marcello?"

"Not personally, no."

I edged closer, dropping my arms on his shoulders, curiosity making my insides buzz. I needed to know everything about the man my dad wanted me to marry. It was the only chance I had to get out of it or make Marcello hate me enough to renege on the deal.

"What *do* you know about him? I'm sure you heard a few things."

Sal didn't answer for a long time. Too long. His foot tapped a steady beat on the floor. The fan whirled overhead. "I should wait downstairs. Your dad won't like it if he comes home and finds me in your room."

"Oh no you don't. Not now." I wrapped my arms around his waist, pulling his back flush with my front and buried my face in his neck. I didn't have any illusions I could prevent him from escaping. I weighed a hundred and five pounds max. He was nearly a foot taller than me, and he had all those muscles that had the habit of making themselves known even beneath a suit. "Tell me what you know. Please. I haven't been able to piece anything together. It's like he's a ghost, and it doesn't help that I didn't even know his real name until now."

Sal reached back and smoothed a hand down my back, his fingers getting lost in the tangles of my messy hair. "In all honesty, I don't know much, other than that he has a lot of power. Some say he's next in line to be the head of the Masciantonio

Family. Some think he doesn't have anything to do with them anymore. If I remember correctly, he's in his twenties, maybe early thirties. I don't know. He's kind of a mystery."

I drew his woodsy scent into my lungs and rubbed my forehead against the prickle of his five o'clock shadow. "What else?"

"He beat a rap for fraud and loan-sharking six or so years ago. I think he was a soldier even though his dad was the boss. Nobody believed he had a future because he had a hot temper. After the jury acquitted him, things changed. He developed a knack for negotiating the outfit out of sticky situations, and that earned him a lot of respect. He has a shit ton of power in Chicago, and not only in the criminal world."

My stomach soured, and I tightened my hold on him like he could somehow change my fate. "My dad doesn't know, but I met him once. Or at least I think I did."

I squeezed my eyes shut, fighting the memory of meeting Marcello. It surfaced anyway.

CHAPTER ELEVEN

Loud voices woke me up, and I crept down the stairs to make sure my dad was okay. My mom and dad had been fighting all the time. I was worried about him, especially since she had disappeared on another trip.

When I reached the alcove outside of the study, I ducked inside to listen.

"It's a done deal," barked a man's voice I didn't recognize, and my nerves shimmered with anxiety.

"I'm sure there's something I can offer you to change your mind," my dad shot back.

"Not interested in what you have to offer."

"I'll give you forty percent."

"Why would I share it when it will all be mine anyway?"

"She might refuse you."

"Then she refuses me. This isn't about the money. This is about what you did to my family and my godfather, and unlike you, I'm a man of word. My family made a promise, and I intend to honor it."

"Don't talk to me like that." The booming sound of a fist hitting wood echoed into the hall. *"I knew you when you were a little shit in diapers, and I've heard enough about your reputation to know you're not good for my daughter just like your father wasn't good enough for Ava."*

"I'm done wasting my time on this. I'm going to marry your daughter like everyone agreed, so you better get used to the idea of having me as your son-in-law and treat me with the respect I deserve, or I'll turn her against you, and you'll be left with no one. They'll both hate you."

I blanched, and my body curled into itself. Marry this stranger? What the hell was going on?

The sound of breaking glass exploded inside of the room and I flinched.

"Don't fuck with me. You won't like the consequences."

"No, I won't be fucking with you. As I understand it, I'll be fucking your daughter."

I gasped at the crude exchange, quickly slapping a hand over my mouth. I was thirteen, but I'd be the first to admit I lived in a bubble of my dad's creation.

The study door flung open, then closed immediately, slamming against the doorframe and rattling the wall. The stranger ran his hand through his dark hair. Shadows hid his face, but I didn't need to see him to sense the power emanating from him. He was the type of man who strutted into a room and owned it and everyone in it without uttering a single word. My breaths came out in ragged pants, and whole body shivers overtook me.

I silently prayed he wouldn't look in my direction.

He sauntered toward the front door, all loose-limbed elegance like he didn't have a care in the world, and he didn't give a shit that my dad had threatened him. Most men would curl into a ball and beg for forgiveness. Not him, and that fascinated me despite all of his obnoxious words.

His hand curled around the handle and halted mid-motion, turning his head to me. He closed the distance between us, his unearthly eyes never veering from mine. He towered over me in his expensive, tailored suit. I experienced a weird sensation of familiarity, like I knew him or should know him.

"You're Emilia."

I nodded, my throat too dry to summon a response.

His gaze sharpened on my thin white t-shirt and sleep shorts and I felt some unexplainable combination of excitement and discomfort. "You're a little thing, aren't you?"

I folded my arms across my chest. "Who are you?"

One side of his mouth hitched up, and he kissed my cheek. An irresistible impulse to be closer to him sparked through me, and I curled my hands around the sleeves of his smooth jacket, inhaling his masculine scent.

"Your future."

Almost as if his words marked the moment my entire world shifted on its axis, the floor whirled beneath my bare feet, and I tightened my hold on him.

"I don't even know you," I whispered into his chest.

He chuckled, the sound bottomless and dancing with a hint of amusement, and his chest vibrated against me. He tipped up my chin, his eyes as blue as the darkest sapphire. "We know each other, Little Emilia."

I shook my head in denial. "No."

"Yes," he answered, stepping out of my reach and striding out of the door.

I hadn't seen him since.

CHAPTER TWELVE

"Emilia?" Sal's voice drew me out of the memory that had plagued me for years, especially because my mom killed herself less than a month later. "Are you okay?"

"Yeah. Sorry about that. I was thinking about that night."

"Why do you believe it was Marcello?"

I swallowed. "The man said something about being my future."

His arms tightened around me. "What else did he say?"

"I don't remember, and it doesn't matter because I won't marry him. I want to marry someone I love. Someone far away from this life. That's what my mom wanted. She fought my dad to leave and take me with her. She wanted me to have choices. He won."

"What you mean? Didn't she kill herself?" I flinched, and Sal gathered me onto his lap, his hands cupping my face, forcing me to look him in the eye. "Shit, Em, I'm sorry for saying that. It was stupid."

"You don't need to apologize." I rested my forehead against his chest. "That's the story, only I'm not sure it was that clear cut. They were fighting for months. She left for a week and when she came back, the friction between them was worse than ever. I could hear her yelling at him from upstairs. After an hour, everything was eerily silent. I assumed they finally worked everything out. I was wrong. An ambulance showed up an hour later, and my dad forbade me from leaving my room. I never saw her again. I never even got the chance to say goodbye except to the urn in my dad's study. I'm pretty sure that doesn't count."

"I know it sounds stupid, but I don't know what to believe. That's part of the reason I want out of here. I can't look at my dad without wondering if he pushed her t-to…" I closed eyes and rolled my lips into my mouth, pain spreading under my breastbone like wildfire. I wasn't surprised. I couldn't think about that night without wanting to crawl into a ball and cry for everything I lost in a matter of hours. My mom, my dad, my family. My life changed in the blink of an eye and everything I loved disappeared, even my dad. He was a different person after she died.

"I know, Em. You don't need to say it. I get that saying things out loud makes them real."

I changed the subject, attempting to reverse the melancholy direction of my reflections. "Anyway, the thing with Marcello, well, that was one of the reasons I asked you to kiss me on my birthday. I'd never kissed anyone before, and I didn't want my first kiss to be with some stranger who could care less about me beyond my last name and what that gets him. You know, kind of like a rebellion against my dad and the curiosity of kissing someone all rolled into one."

He studied me, desire carved into every line of his face, and I couldn't look away. My heart fluttered like a million ants marching against my chest, and an unsolicited flare of heat licked at my nerve endings. I felt like a leaf caught in the wind, blowing from one emotion to the next.

"Oh, yeah?" he murmured, his voice gruff. His eyes scrunched up at the corners, softening like molten lava. He brushed his fingers over my lower lip. "And did it meet your expectations?"

"Yeah." My response was so hushed, I wasn't confident he heard me.

His warm breath puffed across my face, lingering. Teasing. My obsession with him came roaring back to life. A whimper composed of relief and despair sprang from my mouth.

"Are you going to kiss me again?" I whispered, hiking up my chin, shyly offering myself to him.

"I shouldn't."

"But do you want to?"

He licked his lower lip. "More than anything."

I lowered my eyelids, and he went for it. His lips swept against mine. Once. Then twice. At first, it was more of a way to comfort me than anything else. That quickly changed. With every touch of his lips, my pulse surged until I was certain it was audible to the outside world.

Exhaling, I leaned back, deliberating how to end

this before he hurt me again. The second my eyes connected with Sal's, I knew I had overestimated my capacity to resist his lure. His hooded eyes and parted lips only made want to leap right back into whatever insanity held me captive for months.

He didn't give me time to dissect my next move or burgeon my resolve. In a matter of seconds, his fingers tangled in my hair, his full lips on mine again. Demanding, inviting, and frantic, like he feared I'd dematerialize if he stopped. Like he was apologizing for keeping me at arm's length for months.

Part of me wondered if my recently traumatized mind created this fantasy and I'd wake up from a deep slumber only to be alone and craving Sal more than ever. Yet, when his hands started exploring my body freely, I couldn't bring myself to care. Whatever this was—illusion or reality—I'd take it and bask in the feeling of being wanted by this man until it ended.

His hand teased the sliver of skin between my shirt and jeans, and goose bumps dotted my arms. I parted my lips and let him inside. He devoured me like tomorrow would never come and we were the only two people who mattered. He tasted like freedom, fate, and home all wrap up in one wicked package. I dumped every emotion into the kiss— fear, want, longing and lust.

Seconds, minutes, or hours later, I didn't have a clue, he was on top of me, his muscular frame flattening me into the bedding. His hips moved against me and I wrapped my legs around his waist, doggedly ignoring the warning bells ringing nonstop in my brain.

His lips journeyed down my jaw to my neck, and I brushed aside of all of the horrific things that happened today and focused on him, his soft lips, his calloused hands, his heady scent.

"God, Em, do you know how bad I've wanted to kiss you again? It's been torture staying away from you. The minute I saw you in that cabinet in your dad's office with that half-scared, half-defiant look on your face, I wanted you. Every time I pushed you away, it killed me."

My heart swelled at a maddening rate, irrationally hungry for every kiss and every whispered confession. I was an addict gobbling up his words like they were my next fix.

"I didn't ask you to stay away." I hooked my arms around his neck. "You did that all on your own."

His head dropped, resting against the center of my chest. "I know. I didn't have a choice. You know what your dad would do if he found out..." His voice faltered, but he didn't need to finish his sentence. We both knew what he was getting at, and the awareness of this hard reality was as potent as a bucket of ice. Rubbing a hand through his hair, he crawled off the bed. "I need to go before we do something we can't take back. This isn't supposed to happen like this. Your dad wanted...never mind."

I opened my mouth, only I didn't get the chance to argue with him. My dad's voice rang out, and his heavy footfalls echoed on the stairs. "Emilia? Emilia! Where are you?"

"See even fate agrees." Sal heaved out a

weighted breath and opened my door. "She's in here. She just finished eating, and now that you're home, I'm gonna take off."

He walked out of the room without a backward glance, and somehow, in a twisted turn of events, Sal had me thinking about him rather than what happened today. Then it hit me with the force of a bulldozer. I liked Sal. I liked him a lot. My infatuation with him hadn't gone anywhere, and I had no business feeling anything about anyone connected to the Trassato Crime Family. I need to cut the tentacles linking me to them, not grow new ones.

Merda!

CHAPTER THIRTEEN

"Do you want to talk about what happened the other day?" My dad's coffee mug clunked against the long wooden table.

Avoiding eye contact with him, I dug my spoon through my cereal, the little O's spinning in circles, kind of like my thoughts. "No, not really."

He grunted and reared back in his chair, his arms folded across his chest and his lips pursed. "Emilia, we need to talk about it. I didn't push you that night or the last two days because I could see you weren't ready, but it's time."

"Look, Dad, I understand what I'm supposed to do. Sal already talked to me about it. He said I should move on, forget it ever happened, and that's what I'm doing. I don't want to talk about it. I don't want to think about it. I want to pretend it didn't happen, and I'm sure that's what you want too, so we're all good. No need for a conversation."

I dropped my spoon onto the table, my appetite vanishing like a mirage in the desert. I couldn't summon the will to do anything other than stare absently as my mind replayed the events of that day on a continuous reel.

While I understood Sal's point about those guys being bad people, it didn't diminish the queasiness swirling inside my gut for days. I watched two men bleed out and die. I'd scoured the internet looking for any signs their death wasn't a figment of my imagination, and I couldn't find a single thing. It was like the whole incident never occurred. Tony must be one helluva a cleaner, because two men lost their lives and the world kept going like they were never a part of it in the first place, kind of like my mom. With that realization, the little bites of cereal threatened to reverse course and come back up like a bunch of ugly secrets refusing to kick the bucket.

"Emilia, I know our relationship has been…" he paused, his dark eyes distant, "…strained over the last few years. I want things to change."

I barely curbed the urge to roll my eyes. "And how do you want to go about changing things between us?"

"We can start by communicating openly. For example, you tell me what happened with Sal, and I'll explain what I can."

"You know what? I'll humor you even though you're well aware of everything that went down. Sal stopped at some warehouse on the way home. I made the mistake of getting out of the car when I heard a gunshot, and I'm pretty sure you know everything after that."

He steepled his fingers in front of his face, his eyes boring into me with the force of a laser. "Yeah, yeah, I got that part. Did either of the men say anything unusual?"

Unusual? Was he serious? How was I supposed to know what was out of the ordinary for someone to say while threatening to kill a person? "Um, no."

"There has to be something. Sal's been unusually tight-lipped about the whole thing."

I rubbed my temples, my brain feeling like it would explode any minute. "I don't know. Oh wait, one of the men mentioned you honoring some bargain. Then he brought up Sal's dad, and that seemed to set him off. He claimed to have information about Sal's dad, and I guess Sal didn't believe him because he shot him instead of trying to get it out of him. I don't know if that means anything to you, but that's all I've got."

"Okay, sweetheart. That's fine. I don't want to push you too hard. I love you. I know I don't tell you often enough, but it's true." He stood and kissed my cheek. I couldn't remember the last time my dad showed me any affection.

I nodded, stubbornly willing away the urge to cry. "I love you too." It wasn't a lie. I did love him despite the fact that he made my mom so miserable she felt like she didn't have any choice except to end her life. Part of me wished I hated him. It would make my life much easier because loving him as much as I loathed him tore me apart.

He smiled without it reaching his eyes. While I liked to believe I wasn't that transparent, maybe I was.

"You look so much like your mom these days. So much so that I think I'm seeing her ghost roaming around these halls." He pressed a balled up fist to his chest. "Sometimes I wonder if you got any of my genes. I miss her."

"Yeah, I do too." My voice was much rougher than I liked. I didn't want to show any weakness around my dad. He always had an agenda, and I'd be dumb to think he didn't have one right now.

"I know you blame me for what happened. We were fighting all day. I'm sure you overheard some of our conversation."

I nodded, unable to speak. Almost by unspoken agreement, we never discussed that night. About a month after she died, I brought it up he shut me down immediately and refused to talk to me for an entire month. I never made that mistake again. It marked the beginning of the end of our relationship. After that, we orbited around each other, never actually connecting on any level, and neither of us had made any effort to change that until today.

"It's no secret that your mom wanted her old life back. She missed performing in front of crowds and traveling all over the world. She said she felt meaningless and small when she couldn't share her gift with the world. She wanted a different life for both of you, and when she realized it was impossible, she gave up."

An all too familiar ache burrowed under my breastbone, and my shoulders drooped from the weight of his words. They weren't new. I heard them straight from her mouth on more than one occasion, and I'd spent more than a couple of nights turning them over in my head. Even half a decade later, I couldn't come to terms with them or what happened later. I never accepted that my mom willingly chose death over a life of being my mom. That was one of the extensive list of the reasons I suspected my dad pushed her in that direction or bullied her into it.

"I know. I heard what she said."

He tugged on the hem of his suit jacket and dropped his gaze to the dark stained hardwood floors. "Know that she's proud of you. So proud. When you play the piano," he cleared his throat, "it takes my breath away. Just like her."

"Thanks." At a loss for words, I avoided his weighty surveillance.

He patted me on the shoulder. "Anyway, I talked to your piano teacher and she said you have a performance this weekend. I've cleared my schedule so I can be there for you."

I looked up. "You're coming?"

My heart beat double time. My dad hadn't come to a single performance since my mom died. Apparently, he had my teacher tape them, and he listened to them at his leisure.

"I will." He shifted his weight. "By the way, what do you think of Sal?"

I blinked not understanding his question. "Salvatore D'Amico? What about him?"

"Are you comfortable around him?"

I tilted my jaw to the side, trying to read between the lines. "Yes."

"More so than Tony?"

"He's closer to my age, so I feel like I'm hanging out with a friend and not being chaperoned."

"And that's all it is, friendship?"

My stomach squeezed. He'd kill Sal if he knew

he kissed me. "Yes. Sal treats me like a sister. That's it. He doesn't see me as anything more. I'm not sure he even likes me much."

My dad's steely gaze pinned me in place, and my heart rate kicked up a few notches. "Okay. Good. You'd tell me if there was anything going on, right?"

I willed away the heat inching up my neck. "Yeah, of course. Why?"

"Tony's busy with some other project so Sal will be filling in for him from now on. I think you two will be good for each other. He lost his dad a while ago so you have some stuff in common."

"Oh, all right." I ducked my chin to hide my smile. "Whatever you think. I trust you."

CHAPTER FOURTEEN

I smoothed the wispy layers of my pale pink dress, wishing I picked something less conspicuous. I couldn't recall the last time I dressed in any color other than black. Rather than being confident and feeling pretty in my new dress, I felt like a warped version of Tinkerbell.

Closing my eyes, I concentrated on the announcer giving a brief history of my training and mentioning my mom. I wished they wouldn't link the two of us together before a performance. It only increased the already overwhelming pressure to live up to her legacy.

Polite clapping reached my ears, signaling it was time for my entrance. With unsteady legs, I crossed the hardwood floor, my low heels tapping with each step. Next to the bench, I dipped in a semblance of a curtsy and settled onto the bench in front of the gleaming black lacquered piano.

My eyes scanned the front row, seeking the seat where I expected to find my dad, only I didn't. Instead, my gaze met Sal's. His lips pulled up at the corners, and he nodded. The gesture of encouragement was wasted on me. The smile slipped from my face almost immediately. My dad had broken his promise. He didn't come. My lips wobbled, and I flattened a hand against my stomach, willing away the sensation of being kicked in the gut. I knew better than to count on him.

Shake it off. You'll be gone soon anyway.

I took a deep breath, my bodice stretching tight over my ribcage, lowered my hands to the keys, and closed my eyes. My feet found the pedals, and I tapped them three times for good luck then began. The ivory keys gave way under the light pressure of my fingertips. Soft music filled my ears, and with it the ball in my stomach unknotted, succumbing to the meditative tone of the beginning of "Moonlight" by Beethoven.

I moved through each part of the piano sonata, the music building, and the contemplative nature gradually exploding into something promising, then stormy. Passionate. Alive. The strongly accented notes at the end bordered on lyrical, drawing a notable contrast to the first part. My fingers moved faster and faster until I struck the last notes, bowing in reverence for the piece. Sweat beaded near my hairline, my hands vibrated with adrenaline, and the applause rippled like a drug through my body.

I loved performing. It helped me forget all the outrageous crap going on in my life. Most importantly it made me feel close to my mom. Part of me imagined her there watching over me, shaking her head where I missed a note and smiling in encouragement when I pulled off a particularly difficult piece.

When the clapping faded away, I rose from the bench and headed for the side of the stage. With each step, the endorphins dried up, yielding to my frustration. Fortunately it didn't last long. Sal gathered me into his arms a few minutes after I snuck around the black curtain.

"I don't know much about piano, but I have no words, Emilia. You're amazing. Absolutely amazing."

I chuckled. "I'll ignore the qualifier at the beginning of your compliment and run with the second part."

He pulled a bouquet of white roses with a blue ribbon from a canvas bag sitting next to his feet. From the looks of it, he had stuffed a couple of peacock feathers into the arrangement. At some point, I needed to confess that birds freaked me out. "These are from your dad. He's…uh…he couldn't make it. I guess something came up at the club that required his input. He promised he'd make it to the next one."

Determinedly ignoring the feathers, I gathered the flowers in my hand, inhaled their sweet scent, making sure they didn't touch my face, then let them dangle limply from my fingers. "You don't have to lie for him. He hasn't made it to any of my performances since my mom died. I got his message loud and clear. I don't understand why he insists I continue playing when he doesn't want anything to do with it."

Sal shifted on his feet, the slight narrowing of his eyes and his downturned lips broadcasting his discomfort with the conversation. I decided to let him off the hook. He came here and watched the performance. He was one more guest than I usually had. That said enough.

"Don't worry, Sal. I'm not asking you to confirm or deny anything. I'm glad you're here. Usually the seats reserved for my family remain vacant." I lifted the roses to my nose one more time, checking the urge to shiver, because no joke, feathers were gross. I mean, they were the equivalent of plucking hair off someone's head and using it for decoration. "By the way, I know these are from you and not my dad. There's no way the thought crossed his mind to get flowers."

Sal's gaze flickered to the side. "You ready to go? I made dinner reservations. Your dad said there's a restaurant you like a couple of blocks away."

"Miss Trassato? Miss Trassato?" My piano teacher burst through the cliques of people. I had no clue why she insisted we use our last names when speaking to each other after ten years of weekly lessons. I made a few attempts to undermine her desire for formality, and it freaked her out so I backed off. There were only so many people and things I could fight in my life, and my piano teacher wasn't one of them. My dad took up most of my energy.

"Mrs. Vitali, did something happen?"

Her dark eyes bounced all over the place, an overly bright smile on her face that came across as painful. "Don't worry. It's all good news. Mr. Corriere wants to discuss a position at the San Luigi music conservatory in Italy. He flew all this way to listen to you play. Can you believe it?" At my blank look, she explained, "It's a very prestigious school. You should be excited about this, and if my memory serves me, your mother went there too."

She waved her stick-like arm and a man with midnight colored hair, golden skin, and a dark suit stepped forward. "This is Mr. Corriere. He'd like a few moments of your time. Another one of my students is performing, so I need to run, but you'll be fine. He was very impressed with you."

Mrs. Vitali hurried away, leaving me face to face with this man. My cheeks heated under his intense onceover. While I waited for him to say something, the air around me grew thick with anticipation and crackling nerves. I wasn't used to being around men outside of my father's circle of acquaintances and family.

"Miss Trassato." He pressed a kiss to each of my cheeks, his spicy cologne engulfing me.

"Nice to meet you, Mr. Corriere."

A smile spread across my face. It was like God hadn't forgotten me after all, and hand-delivered a way to sidestep a marriage to Master Marcello, or whatever the heck his name was. The best part was that my dad couldn't get mad at me. He'd been pushing me toward this goal all of my life.

"*Piacere*, and call me Lorenzo." His voice was low and slightly accented, rolling over my bare arms like warm syrup. Objectively speaking, he was an attractive man, a little over six feet tall with silver threading the sides of his otherwise dark hair. The creases around his eyes and mouth testified to a life filled with laughter, good food, and wine.

"This is Sal D'Amico."

I waved my hand in Sal's direction, and he stepped forward, gripping Lorenzo's hand in a firm grasp. His knuckles whitened, his lips thinned, and I saw the gesture for what it was—a warning shot.

"Nice to meet you," Sal grunted out, looking a little irritated.

"Emilia, may I call you Emilia?"

I nodded. "Of course."

"You've been on our radar for years, and we'd like to officially offer you a position at San Luigi." He pulled an envelope out of his black leather briefcase and handed it to me. "All the details are inside. While I'm confident you'll find the offer to your liking, we can discuss the details over dinner."

"Um, well…" I would have loved to dive into this feet first, but I had a lot to consider before I could enter into serious discussions with this man.

Sal edged forward, throwing his arm around my shoulder. "Emilia has dinner plans, but she'll look over the details and get back with you. Your contact information is inside, right?"

Sal's face was all hard, unforgiving angles, his jaw muscles working overtime, a complete one-eighty from his greeting after the performance.

"I leave tomorrow, and I will be traveling for a couple of weeks, so it has to be tonight."

"Emilia needs to run this by her father before she can arrange a meeting."

I took in a deep breath, tamping down the compulsion to contradict Sal and cause a scene. This wasn't his business even if my dad had appointed him as my official chaperone after the incident at the warehouse. Sal kept me safe that day, so my dad rewarded him by sticking him on daughter duty. I couldn't complain when it meant I got to see Sal nearly every day and I liked him. A lot. Even if he hadn't so much as touched me inappropriately since that night in my room.

"She's over eighteen, no?" Lorenzo shot back, the vein at his temple throbbing. "She can make her own decisions, and the offer includes a full scholarship, along with living expenses, so there's not much to consider. Her needs will be taken care of."

My heart vaulted against my chest. I wanted to scream *yes* at the top of my lungs. The offer bordered on being too good to be true. While I was an accomplished pianist, I didn't have any notoriety outside of New York. I've never performed anywhere that would draw international interest, and that alone made me hesitate to come right out and accept the offer.

"Excuse us for a second. I need to talk to Emilia in private," Sal announced, already hauling me across the room by my wrist.

"You overbearing *ciuccio*...Oh, I can't *believe* you dragged me away like I'm incapable of...of..." I sputtered, seething. I glared at him for a long time, unable to form a coherent response.

"Em, listen to me," he implored, his arms coming around me.

"No, you listen to me. I don't need you telling me what options I can consider. I have a father to do that, and trust me, he doesn't let me make a single decision by myself, and I'm starting to think you'll turn out to be worse than him."

He scoffed. "You can handle me. Compared to your dad, I'm a walk in the park. I don't have any ulterior motives. What you see is what you get." With every word, his mouth brushed against my ear, and his hands skated up and down my upper arms. A shiver rolled through me.

"Yeah, I'm not that stupid. I know you're not as straightforward as you seem. You have secrets. You have motives. Everyone does, and you're no different. I just haven't figured out what your angle is yet."

His calloused hands sunk in the back of my hair, and he tipped my face upward, forcing me to meet his eyes. His thumbs moved in a circular pattern near my temples. "Think about this for a second without going off half-cocked. Your dad would kill me if I let you go to dinner with some man without his permission, and I'm pretty sure he'd lock you in your room for weeks. You know how particular he is about accounting for your time. I'm not blind. I see how much you want this, but pissing off your dad right now isn't the way for you to go about getting it."

In my heart, I acknowledged the truth in his words, and it scared me. Would I ever be free of my father? Maybe I was spinning my wheels here. I could run away, join the circus, accept this scholarship, and none of it mattered. My father would always be right around the corner, sucking me back into his life and everything that came along with being at the center of the Trassato Crime

Family. The restrictions, the expectations—all of it conspired to enslave me and permanently chain me to a future I didn't want.

"I know." I rested my forehead against his chest. "I want out so bad, and this might be the simplest way to go about it."

"Out of what?"

"This life. The Trassato family duty stuff. The marriage my dad's negotiating. All of it. If I jump on this opportunity, my dad might be mad. He can't do anything, though, because it's harmless. I'm following my dream. The same dream he's jammed down my throat since my mom died, and if everything works out, I might never have to come back here or marry that guy I don't know. It's perfect."

He tightened his hold on me for a split second, the roses flattening between our bodies. "Okay, Em, I get it. I do, and I'll help you. It can't go down like this. We have to be smart about it. You need to break it to your dad first and let him think he's in control, otherwise he'll shut this down so fast your head will spin. And I hate to point out the obvious, but we need to research this guy before you commit to anything. Using you would be the perfect set up to get to your dad."

A shuddery groan tore from my lips, my mind whirling with the implications. The fact he said "we" not "you" stuck out like a blinking, neon sign, and I liked that a whole lot more than I'd ever admit. Since my mom died, nobody was on my team. While I didn't want to read too much into Sal's words, I couldn't deny they made me feel all warm and fuzzy deep in my belly, kind of like a shot of grappa.

"Yeah, you're right. I'll go tell Lorenzo I'll be in touch after I review the materials and discuss it with my family."

He brushed a few teasing kisses on my lips, and my heart stalled for a flash. He hadn't kissed me since that night after the warehouse incident, and sometimes I wondered if I imagined the whole thing.

I curled one of my hands into the tight weave of his suit and the other in the short hair on the back of his skull, not wanting to let go of him and this moment yet. Who knew how long I'd have to wait until I felt his mouth against mine again. He ran hot and cold—well, a little less cold lately, and more mysterious. I couldn't get a read on what he wanted from me, if anything at all.

His mouth skated hot across my jaw, and he nuzzled the hollow beneath my ear. Incomprehensible warmth traveled through me, and I sagged against the solid planes of his chest, the steady thump of his heart beneath the palm of my hand. His relatively innocent kiss lit me up like a stick of dynamite.

"I'll wait here while you talk to him. Then we'll go."

CHAPTER FIFTEEN

We didn't go out to dinner, and the conversation with Lorenzo quickly vanished from my mind when I discovered Sal's intended destination. My legs teetered, and my heart galloped, both nervous and excited to be alone with Sal at his studio apartment.

I'd tried to keep my feelings for him in check, not wanting to get my hopes up or read anything into his kisses, his lingering touches, or the way his eyes followed me from place to place like he had less than honorable intentions. It was an uphill battle, and it wasn't long before stage five clinger thoughts rambled nonstop through my mind.

I cleared my throat. "So what are we doing here? I can't imagine that this is on my dad's list of approved destinations. These days he only lets me out of the cage to go to family events and piano lessons. I take that back. He did let me do lunch with Lettie that one day way back when, but that doesn't count."

Sal peeled off his suit jacket and unknotted his tie. His eyes gleamed with so many layers and unspoken intentions that my toes curled inside my heels. Giddiness and want coiled around my chest, fogging up my brain. The all too familiar draw of Sal sucked me under like quicksand, and I knew I was a goner. I'd follow him to the end of the Earth right now if he asked. He threaded his fingers through mine and led me to the worn black leather sofa, pulling me into his lap.

"Well, the performance won't end for another hour and a half so I figured we had some time to kill."

My heart kicked up a notch. Sal's startling eyes studied me, his lids dipping lower and his lips inching upward. Since that night in my room, I couldn't stop reminiscing about the way his hands and lips felt against my skin. I'd spent my entire life in the cocoon of my dad's making, only breaking out a slight amount recently, and I wanted more.

I fidgeted with my hands in my lap, not sure where to put them. His thighs? His shoulders? "Uh-huh," I mumbled, knowing he expected an answer.

"We are going to have dinner. They're delivering it here in an hour. The question is what are we going to do until then?"

I knew what I wanted to do. I wanted nothing more than to close my eyes and get hopelessly lost in him. Every time Sal touched me or kissed me, I tasted freedom. Freedom from my life, from my dad's rules, and freedom from the future looming over my life like a heavy storm cloud ready to burst. The scholarship to the San Luigi music conservatory was akin to a one-way ticket out of this hell. Before I took it, I wanted to explore this mystifying connection with Sal, damn the consequences.

I couldn't hold back any longer. I needed to touch him again, especially now that I knew I could be gone in a matter of months. I raised my hand, leaving it suspended next to his head for a beat, deliberating, deciding. I pushed the pads of my fingers through his silky brown locks. The light rippled through his hair, bringing out strands of gold, copper, and coffee all plaited together to create the complex brown.

His hand looped over one of my knees, separating them fractionally, and heat flared between my legs. He tipped up his chin, more or less daring me to act on what was written all over my face. Giving into the temptation, I touched the sharp angle of his jawline, his five o'clock shadow abrading my fingers as they made their way to his mouth. I planted my pinkie finger in the center of that dent in his lower lip.

Rather than coming right out and saying what I wanted, I shrugged. Sal had to spell out what he wanted because his mixed signals had me turning in circles. "It's up to you."

"Oh, yeah." His hand closed around my arm, pulling me closer, our noses brushing. "In that case…" His mouth met mine with a staggering amount of passion, and it only took seconds to unravel my inhibitions. We bit, nipped, dueled, dancing around what we wanted to happen. He tasted like the coffee candy he popped in his mouth on the way here.

Tension wove through my body muscle-by-muscle, and the sensation of my limbs folded over him made me a little woozy in the best possible way. I pressed my legs together, his hand still wedged between them, a reminder of where this would go if I had my way. I was ready to break all of the invisible chains my father had wrapped around me since my mom's death.

My hands hooked around his firm shoulders, savoring the feel of his sturdiness, his competence. Sal reached around my back, unzipping my dress. The soft humming noise echoed in my ears, and my eyes widened, panic bubbling up in my chest. Instinctively, I clutched the front of my dress, and my other hand circled his wrist, gripping the sensitive skin on the underside.

He paused, the pads of his fingers unhurriedly stroking my back. "I only want to see you. Touch you. Make you feel good. I'll even keep my clothes on so it doesn't go too far. Are you okay with that?"

I nodded and released my hold on the front of my dress. It fell to my waist and his breath caught.

"Beautiful," he whispered, so softly I damn near missed it.

His knuckles brushed across the tips of my breasts, pushing the long strands of my hair over my shoulder. Then his palms cupped the mounds, his lips moving across my jaw and down my neck.

I tensed a little, and he murmured soft, soothing noises. Gradually, I bloomed beneath his touches, my confidence growing second by second until I felt safe and free to explore him and allow myself to luxuriate in the sensations rippling through my body without guilt.

One second he was guiding me backward and the next he blanketed me, pressing me into the sagging cushions. One of his hands tangled in my hair, gripping and pulling at it like he wanted to crawl inside of me.

His hand slipped under the hem of my pale pink dress. My nerve endings buzzed with the unknown, and my pulse accelerated. He toyed with the edge of my panties, and my heart bounced around inside of my chest like a bowling ball. All the while, he kept kissing and nibbling. Unhinged ideas whipped through my brain, none of them making much sense except the overarching theme for him to continue with whatever he was doing.

One finger pushed inside my panties, and I nearly came out of my skin. Air exploded out of my lungs in ragged, needy breaths that burned a path up my throat. My fingernails dug into the sleeves of his white dress shirt like I could melt the delicate barrier between us if I pressed hard enough.

His long, calloused fingertip found my center, sliding in circles like he owned me. My uncertainty and reservations evaporated. I gasped, my hips arching off the sofa. All sense of reality slipped away until it was only the two of us and the game-changing sensation building inside of me. It was like nothing I'd ever felt before. Sure, I'd experimented, touching here or there, but it was like fumbling in the dark compared to this.

My body pulsed, silently begging for a reprieve. His warm breath spilled across my neck as his honeyed voice told me how much he wanted me, how he couldn't stay away from me, how he couldn't tear his eyes away from me on the stage, how perfect I felt in his arms, and so many other things. I couldn't process each of them.

"Sal…please," I rasped, not even sure what I wanted. He knew, though. His hand moved faster, curling upward. My mind whirled, the tension inside of me on the brink of becoming unbearable. Then a white blaze of light detonated behind my eyelids. My muscles tensed, and my toes curled. A moan smothered by a cry split my lips, and he kept going until the tingling sensation died out.

I went limp, and he buried his head in the crook of my neck. "Jesus, Emilia. That was…" His kissed the underside of my ear.

"I know," I finished for him because all I could think about was starting over from the beginning again, and committing each sensation to memory so I'd never forget it.

A knock sounded at the door, and Sal sat up, gently putting my dress back in place. "That's probably the food. I'll answer it and get everything ready while you finish getting dressed. We don't have much time to eat before I need to drive you home."

"Wait." I grabbed his silver belt buckle, my hands trembling. "I want to do something for you too. I could touch you or something else."

"Not tonight." He scrambled to his feet, putting a solid five feet between us. "This was about you. I don't want…" He ran his hand through his already messy hair. "Let's stop while we're ahead."

I licked my lips, watching the rapid rise and fall of his chest. "Why not? I know I'm inexperienced, but isn't that what normally happens?"

"Because..." He grabbed his suit jacket and stuffed his arms in the sleeves. "We can't let things go too far, and if you keep looking at me like that, I'll forget all the reasons why touching you is a terrible idea. Marcello and your dad..." He swallowed. "This won't end well."

A knock thudded against the door again. Defeat swarmed inside of me. He was right. Until the moment I figured out my life and severed my connection to my father, my future didn't belong to me.

"Then why do anything at all? After my birthday, you turned into a giant asshole, then all of a sudden you like me. I don't get it? Why the change of heart?"

He sighed heavily and scrubbed his hand down his face. "When I'm around you, I don't care about the consequences, but we need to be smart about this. Both of us have a lot to lose if this blows up in our faces."

"I don't want to stop this. Whatever it is."

His hands swallowed the sides of my face, and he kissed me again. I didn't want him to stop. Ever. I couldn't find the words to explain how it felt to be wanted like this after years of being ignored by my family and hidden away from my peers.

"Neither do I, but we can't take this too far. Not yet anyway."

CHAPTER SIXTEEN

I sat at the kitchen table, the envelope Lorenzo gave me wedged between my knees. Nearly an entire week had passed, and I hadn't mustered the courage to discuss the contents with my dad. Mrs. Vitali brought it up at every lesson last week, and I was afraid I was going to be the cause of her early demise if I didn't give her any answer one way or another this afternoon.

All of our conversations to date went the same way. She'd ask if I made a decision. I'd say no and refuse to elaborate. She'd mutter a few words punctuated by a sigh, and I wouldn't lie. Her sighs grated on me. She was one of those uniquely annoying people who wielded sighs rather than words as a weapon. I had to get this over with today for my sanity and hers.

Fingering the already worn corner of the packet, I focused on my dad. His eyes glued to his iPad, he chewed bite after bite of cereal.

Crunch. Crunch. Crunch.

The sound rattled around in my ears, chiding me

to grow some balls and get this over with.

What was the worst that could happen? He could say no. That's all, and then I'd be right back where I started, searching for a way out of the arranged marriage looming over me like the specter of death, only this time I had Sal on my side, and he had promised to help me.

"Dad?" My voice sounded rusty.

He rested his spoon against the side of the bowl, lasering me with his dark eyes, one brow arched in a sharp "v", which was fitting since he often played the villain in my life. "Yes?"

I hadn't so much as uttered more than a single word since he failed to show up at my performance. Tired of balancing on the knife's edge, I swallowed back my fears. I needed to know whether I had a shot at going to San Luigi. A "no" would hurt, but the beating around the bush and living in a dreamlike reality of what-ifs threatened my mental well-being. I needed to rip off the proverbial bandage and face reality.

"A man, Lorenzo Corriere, approached me after my concert." I gathered the envelope and slid it to the middle of the table. "He offered me a position at San Luigi. It's a music conservatory south of Rome. I guess Mom went there. Anyway, the scholarship pays for everything, tuition, room and board, and a small living stipend. It wouldn't cost you anything. I'd love to do this and, you know, follow in Mom's footsteps. I think she would've wanted this for me."

The last part, the part about my mom, was a less than subtle dig at his conscience. If I could persuade my dad this was a good idea, I'd happily throw a little guilt, shame, and blame into the mix to see what would stick. It was the most powerful currency in our world other than money and power.

Without meeting my eyes, he slid out the papers, thumbing through them one after another, though not with enough attention that I actually believed any of the words penetrated his thick skull. No words were exchanged, and I already had my answer. My father would fight this with every dirty trick in his arsenal. He had plans for me, and they didn't include furthering my music career. They stopped and started with marrying some faceless man, popping out a gaggle of kids, and living out the rest of my life in servitude to a man who undoubtedly wanted me as much as I wanted him, which was not at all.

He reached the last page, gathered all the sheets of paper on top of the glossy pamphlet, and straightened them against the top of the table.

Tap. Scrape. Thump.

I flinched with each contact like I was awaiting my execution.

"This is a great opportunity, Emilia. It's more than your mother or I could've imagined when you started banging on those keys in your mom's lap."

A grin split my face, full and wild. I couldn't contain myself, and did a micro hop thing in my chair a few times like I was eight and not eighteen. "I know. Can you believe it? I've been freaking out for days. I can't believe it's real. I've read those papers so many times, I'm pretty sure I know them by heart."

He drummed his fingers on top of the stack. "I

noticed. They look like you've had them for months instead of weeks."

"I was so scared to bring it up with you, so I took my time reading the material and researching the conservatory online. It's so beautiful there, Dad. The buildings are a yellowish stucco with stone and arches everywhere. They're lined with palm trees, and they have a crazy—"

"Emilia." He held up his hand like a big fat red stop sign, and all of my excitement evaporated into bitter ash. "As much as I'd love for you to go here, it can't happen."

My teeth dug into the inside of my cheek with enough force to tinge with my mouth with the metallic taste of blood. "Why not?"

"I was waiting until everything was finalized to tell you this, but I might as well tell you now. I've arranged for you to marry Marcello Masciantonio. He's coming here at Christmas to spend some time with you. He lives in Chicago, which might be a good change of pace for you. You've been in a funk since your mom died, and this move and marriage will give you the chance to reinvent yourself, make new friends and a new life. You can continue your piano lessons if that's what makes you happy or you can start a family. Marcello's talked about that and…"

His words bled together, no longer penetrating my brain. I balled my hands into tight fists, my fingernails tunneling into my palms and more than likely making deep crescents in my flesh. Obviously, his declaration didn't qualify as news. I'd known this had been in the works since the run-in with the man I assumed was Marcello before my mom died, and based on a few recent conversations I overheard, I suspected he intended the marriage to take place in the not too distant future. Consequently, I had upped my efforts to uncover dirt on my dad so I could blackmail him into unwinding the agreement.

Still, his admission, coupled with his refusal to let me attend a renowned music conservatory in Italy, felt like a deathblow. His hate for me had to be enormous. That was the only explanation for his cruelty. What kind of man wanted his daughter to marry a stranger instead of following their dreams?

Sadly, I didn't even realize playing the piano professionally was my dream and not my dad's until Lorenzo approached me. I'd always waffled between loving it and feeling like it was an albatross around my neck. Now that I had the chance to become a concert pianist, I wanted it so bad I could almost taste it.

Silence wrapped around me, thick and stifling, strangling the life out of me one molecule of air at a time. Apparently my dad had ceased explaining himself at some point, and I had failed to react outwardly to his declaration.

"Are you listening to me?" he prompted, in all likelihood noticing my uncomprehending look.

I licked my lips, searching for a suitable evasion. Nothing came to mind, so I settled for the truth. "Yeah, and I don't care what you have to say. I won't be shipped off to another state to marry some random guy because it's good for you or because it gives you more power. I won't be your pawn. Not now. Not ever."

He pinched the bridge of his nose. "This isn't about me. I wish...dammit, Emilia. This is the way it has to be. Trust me. I'm doing everything in my power to protect you, and I will never stop."

"Protect me from what? People who want to hurt you? Great, then let me go to Italy and start a new life where nobody knows anything about me except that I can play the piano with some level of competence. It's the perfect solution. Think about it."

He pushed his chair away from the table, the legs screeching across the floor, frustration etched into every line and angle of his face. "You won't be safe in Italy, and you aren't safe here. Not anymore. I wish there were another option, but I won't lose you too. I can't."

With that parting shot, he exited the room, not bothering to glance back at me.

"You've already lost me," I mumbled, my eyes stinging with the urge to cry.

CHAPTER SEVENTEEN

I stared at the text message from my father summoning me to his study with more than a little disbelief. We hadn't exchanged so much as a word at dinner or anytime in between since he shut down the offer from San Luigi.

Twenty minutes later, I knocked on the thick wood and glass door, hoping he'd changed his mind about wanting to talk to me or he found something more important to do since he sent the text.

"Come in," he said, his voice firm.

I crossed the room and took a seat in the leather chair in front his desk. "Hi, Dad," I said, immediately regretting the weakness of my voice. I stuffed my hands in my pockets to hide the trembling.

He removed his reading glasses from his face and tossed them on top of his desk. "How are things going with Sal?"

My eyes widened, and flames licked at my face. I definitely had to work on my acting skills. "Good. Is something wrong?"

"No. No." He opened a desk drawer, pulled out a square black and white chevron wrapped package, holding it out like a peace offering. "This is for you."

I eyed the package, then him, before taking it from his hand. "You didn't have to get me anything."

"It's not from me. It's from Marcello Masciantonio. I told him I informed you of the marriage, and I guess he felt compelled to send you something."

I dropped it on the desk so fast you'd think someone handed me a package of burning dog crap. "I don't want it. Send it back."

"I can't. Not without offending him and his whole family."

"I don't care about offending them. They don't mean anything to me."

He sighed. "I wish it were that simple, Emilia. Just open the damn present and stuff it in a drawer or donate it to charity. I don't care. You need to learn to pick your battles because not all of them are worth fighting for. Concentrate on the big stuff or you'll run out of energy when it counts."

"Fine. Maybe I'll give it Lettie."

I ripped into the black and white paper and opened the lid on a white box, discarding them on my dad's desk. Inside was a delicate gold cuff bracelet woven with white and black diamonds. My hand hovered over it, desperately wanting to put it on my wrist, but not wanting to show how much I loved it. It was like Marcello, a complete stranger, had climbed into my subconscious and picked out the perfect gift.

Instead of falling prey to its siren call, I reached for the folded piece of paper beneath the bracelet, making sure not to touch it overly long.

Emilia,

This bracelet reminds me of the endless dance between light and darkness, good and evil. One cannot last without the other. They are in everything, including this arrangement. It's all about balance.

Marcello

Rattled, I reread the words five or six times before stuffing the note into my pocket and closing the lid on the bracelet. I needed to be alone to process what he meant, if anything at all.

"What'd he say?"

I met my dad's stare. "Nonsense."

"So is Lettie getting a new bracelet? Unless I'm mistaken, I think he dropped a sizable chunk of change on that thing, and it might make Pietro suspicious."

"Yeah, you're probably right. I'll keep it for now." Truthfully, I'd rather cut off my arm than give it to Lettie. I loved it.

"Did you want to send him a thank you?"

"Oh." I glanced over his shoulder. "I probably should."

I snagged the yellow lined pad of paper and a pen from the corner of the desk.

Marcello,
Thank you for the bracelet. I'm a little confused, though. Which one of us is the light and which one of us is the darkness?
Emilia

I folded it in thirds. "Do you have an envelope?"

He opened his top drawer and handed it to me. "I'll mail it for you."

"Thanks," I said, setting the sealed envelope in his outbox. "Is there anything else you wanted to talk about?"

"That's all."

CHAPTER EIGHTEEN

Over the last four months, Sal had shuttled me to and from my piano lessons twice a week, and we somehow managed to elude my father's watchful eye with enough regularity to feed my Sal addiction. He found hundreds of nearly deserted spots on the route home where we could be together uninterrupted. Most of the time we kissed until my entire body shimmered with need and my nerve endings were zinging like a live wire pleading for more.

Predictably, Sal refused to take our intimacy to the next level. As a matter of fact, he hadn't done anything other than kiss me since that night at his apartment. His constant rejections didn't prevent me from pushing him. He had an absurd amount of willpower because, without fail, every encounter ended with me craving more and him declining to cross some invisible line. We never discussed his reasoning, and frankly, we didn't need to. My engagement party loomed over us like a thunderstorm, especially recently. We both knew if

I couldn't find a loophole to evade the marriage, this thing between us would be over before it went anywhere.

Without a doubt, Marcello wouldn't like the idea of his wife being used goods. The men in our world expected virtue and obedience from their wives. I suspected that was why my father had kept me under lock and key since my mom died. He didn't want anything to taint my future husband's opinion of me. Simply put, I was a commodity to be bought and sold to the highest bidder.

That said, for some reason, my dad trusted Sal, particularly after the incident at the warehouse. It didn't hurt that Sal did everything he could to foster the perception we were platonic friends. Except for the stolen kisses on the way home from piano lessons, he fulfilled my dad's orders flawlessly. In public, he kept a respectful distance, never touching me or looking at me for too long.

Even more frustrating, he always sided with my dad when I pushed to have more of a social life, not that I had people knocking down my door. My friends started and stopped with Lettie, and a call here or there from my cousin Carmela, which seemed more obligatory than anything else.

I understood Sal's rationale for not pushing back against my dad's orders. His deferential behavior allowed us more freedom and kept our relationship under the radar. Increasingly though, I didn't care about the possible ramifications. I wanted to tell anyone who would listen about Sal. I fell for him more with every stolen second spent in his company. As far as I was concerned, Sal owned my heart. He might as well own my body.

My feelings for Sal likely made me the dumbest person on the planet, because the deck was stacked against us, and we couldn't ignore the future much longer. Marcello had made plans to come to my father's annual Christmas Eve party where we'd be formally introduced as a couple, which was only fourteen days away. According to my dad, if everything went well, I'd walk down the aisle shortly after my twentieth birthday like an obedient daughter.

"You're distracted these days." Mrs. Vitali sighed for the hundredth time today. "I don't know why you bother with lessons. Your heart's not in it anymore."

I stuffed my sheet music into my black leather messenger bag. "It's not. My dad won't let me go to the music conservatory so this is a waste of time. If he has his way, I'll be married and pregnant within the next year, and I won't lay a finger on a piano for another decade."

"There has to be something we can do." She pursed her lips and settled her hands on her matronly hips. "You need to continue your lessons in Chicago. I gave you a list of new instructors. You haven't contacted any of—"

I held up my hand, backpedaling to the front door. "We've already talked about this, and I don't have time to get into it again. We've already run fifteen minutes over, and Sal is probably circling the block for the tenth time."

"Fine. However, I'm not giving up on you yet." Another stupid sigh whistled out of her mouth. I should record her so she could hear how ridiculous she sounded. I'd be doing her other students a huge favor. They wouldn't have to learn the art of interpreting a sigh. Or better yet, I could write a handbook. Quick sigh meant disapproval, long sigh meant frustration, and so on.

"See you next week."

I jogged down the steps of her building, a blast of cold afternoon air hitting my cheeks like a slap to the face. I immediately spotted Sal's car idling next to the raised curb. I ducked under a barren tree limb, opened the car door, and practically flung myself into his lap. I buried my nose in the starched collar of his shirt, sucking his scent into my lungs. Nothing smelled better than him.

"I missed you," I mumbled against his neck.

He angled my face upward and captured my lips in a kiss that made me wish we were anywhere but sitting in his car on a busy street in the middle of Brooklyn. With every brush of his lips and swirl of his tongue, the steady hum of traffic and horns faded into nothing. I wanted to crawl inside of him. Needy sounds tumbled from my mouth, and I would have been embarrassed if I didn't believe he felt the same way.

"It's only been seventy-five minutes since I dropped you off."

"I know, but Mrs. Vitali was riding me about wasting my potential and not trying anymore."

He steered the car into traffic. Instead of going straight home after a twenty-minute detour spent kissing Sal per our routine, I was supposed to meet Lettie for dinner. I wished I could cancel on her last minute and spend the next two hours at Sal's house, but he concluded it was too risky. He was right. Lettie was a shameless gossip. She used it as currency to build her relationship with the other wives in the Family. Unfortunately for her, it never worked. They ate up her dirty secrets and ignored her five minutes later. When I tried to explain it to her from my perspective, she didn't care. She was desperate for the acceptance since she'd never get it from her husband or her family.

"I kind of agree with her, ya know? You can't give up on your dream. You don't know what's gonna happen. A lot could change in the next few months."

His voice trailed off, and I could tell he was thinking about Marcello's impending visit.

"I'm not going to marry him regardless what my father does or says."

"I know you don't want to, but what you want might not matter," he said with his casual pragmatism.

Fear pumped through my body as I debated if I should tell him the truth. I took a deep breath and rubbed my hands over the buttery leather upholstery beneath me. I'd been on the fence about confiding in him for weeks, and now I wanted to blurt it out so I could stop speculating about his reaction and whether he'd support me. I held back though. I always held back. Call it survival instinct or fear. Either way, I didn't fully understand it.

"I don't want to talk about it," I replied, chickening out. "My dad agreed to let me do something social, so I'm going to be happy instead of worrying about tomorrow."

He pulled over in front of a fire hydrant. "Is this the restaurant?"

I scrolled through my phone to double check the text from Lettie earlier this morning. "Yep. This is it." I paused. "Oh wait, I guess she couldn't get reservations. I'm supposed to meet her at the park across the street, and then we'll check out a few places from there."

"You're not wandering around alone."

"I won't be alone. I'll be with Lettie." I dropped my phone in the cup holder and retied the laces of my boots. I needed a new pair. The toes were scuffed, and the laces were frayed. My dad had filled my closet full of heels and flats, thinking I'd bend to his demand to dress like a lady. I couldn't do it because somehow the boots had come to represent my metaphorical resistance to him.

"Lettie has her head up her ass half of the time. You'd probably be better off walking the city alone than with her. She invites trouble into her life."

I unclipped my seat belt and cracked open the passenger door. "I don't get it. Why does everyone hate Lettie so much? I feel sorry for her. She was forced to marry Pietro. Her family barely talks to her, and everyone acts like she doesn't exist at parties. I swear I'm the only one who made any effort to get to know her."

"There's a good reason for that."

"So you don't like her either?" I drummed my fingers on my leg. "You lived in her house for nearly a year. She said you were somewhat friendly with each other."

He glanced out the window, his fingers tightening around the steering wheel. "She's a bad influence, and I'd bet my life she doesn't have good intentions when it comes to you."

"Oh, please. You sound like my dad. He warned me away from being anything more than friends with you, and I didn't listen. You know why? Because I'm loyal."

"Look, Em, I don't want to go into the details, but she's not what she pretends to be, and if I had my way, you wouldn't go anywhere near her. She's a selfish bitch. Let's leave it at that. Okay?"

Rage bubbled up in my chest along with all the feelings of helplessness I'd barely managed to keep in check since my father shot down my plea to go to the music conservatory in Italy. I assumed Sal was different. I thought he understood me, only he was like every other man in my life, especially my dad. He wanted to control me and dictate what I could and couldn't do. Well fuck him. I jumped out of the car.

The dam of frustration exploded, and I lashed out. "I can't even do this with you right now. The last thing I need is another man trying to micromanage my life." I slammed the door, the loud clunk ringing in my ears.

Sal rolled down the passenger side window. "Stop acting like a child and get in the fucking car."

"No. Just go, and I'll meet you here in two hours."

"Get in." He leaned across the passenger seat and opened the door.

"No."

116

Horns blared behind him. Drivers shouted obscenities intermixed with colorful hand gestures.

"I'll be fine."

I took off, darting across the street, dodging traffic. Sal sped up, and his tires squealed around the corner. I watched him until his car was out of sight. My stomach swirled with equal amounts of disappointment and relief. I shouldn't have lashed out at him, but after the confrontation with my piano teacher and the mounting pressure of Marcello's visit, I was on edge.

CHAPTER NINETEEN

A swing set surrounded by spindly trees and a few benches sat in the dead center of the park. A stray wrapper rolled near my feet like tumbleweed. The steady hum of traffic was punctuated with a stray dog bark here and there. Except for a man leaning against a tree who stopped to smoke a cigarette a couple of minutes ago, the park was empty.

Dammit, Lettie.

When I reached inside my messenger bag to call her, I groaned. I'd left my phone in the cup holder. Knowing Lettie, she could flake and I wouldn't have a clue. Her husband ran hot and cold. Half the time he barely noticed her, and the other half he meddled in every decision, behaving like a total tyrant, demanding she cancel plans and banning her from leaving the house for weeks on end.

"Shit," I mumbled, burying my face in my hands. I made a mistake coming here. It was getting dark, and Sal wouldn't be back for two hours, if he bothered at all after my stupid temper tantrum. No, he'd come back. Sal could be a jerk, but he wouldn't abandon me somewhere and risk pissing off my dad.

"Having a bad day?" a heavily accented voice rumbled next to my ear. The smell of stale cigarettes wafted across the back of my hair, and two hands landed on my shoulders.

My heart went haywire, and my spine stiffened. I lurched forward, trying to sever this man's hold on me, but it was no use. He tightened his grip and yanked me back into the slats of the metal bench. Before I had the chance to scream, his palm came down on my mouth.

"Shut the fuck up and listen to me," he hissed in my ear.

Panic crawled up my throat and tears burned the corners of my eyes. A sickening concoction of adrenaline swirled in my gut, rendering me blind and deaf to everything aside from the deafening drumming in my ears.

"Miss Trassato?"

The sound of my name rolling off his tongue snapped me out of my imminent panic attack. I jerked my gaze toward him and came face to face with the man who'd been standing across the park a few moments earlier. A fedora hat shadowed his eyes, and a thick beard concealed his features, making him next to impossible to identify in a lineup.

"I'm here to give you a message, not to hurt you. If I release my hand do you promise not to scream?"

I nodded, not sure if I was telling the truth, but needing his hands away from me as fast as possible.

His hand shifted back to my shoulder and he squeezed. Rather than reassuring me of his intentions, the gesture sent a shudder rippling through me, which was probably his intention.

"Now turn around and smile like you've never been happier."

"Who are you?"

"That's not important. I'm only the messenger."

"Then pass on your message and leave me alone.

He chuckled, and the grating sound along with the puff of his breath made my hair stand on end. "Tell your father that *Signor* Bonaccorso sends his regards, and he hasn't forgotten their arrangement."

"What arrangement?"

He buried his hand in my hair, and I arched my back, preparing for him to yank on it. He didn't. "You don't need to worry about the details. He'll understand."

"Hey! What the fuck are you doing?" The sound of Sal's deep voice and his thundering footsteps made my heart sing. I'd never been so relieved in my life.

The man released me and took off in a sprint. Sal grabbed him by the collar of his black trench coat and pulled him to the ground. Arms, legs, and bodies flew in the air, interlaced with the sounds of grunts and flesh meeting flesh. Sal's head whipped sideways, and blood splattered the front of his previously pristine shirt. He didn't waste any time regrouping. He charged, wrapping his arms around the man's waist, forcing him to the ground. Sal straddled him, landing punch after punch.

Sirens sounded in the distance. While I doubted

they were heading here, the noise snapped me out of my stupor. I had to end this before someone called the police or Sal got seriously hurt. I vaulted off the bench, rushing forward. My boots slapped against the gravel, slipping and sliding in my haste to reach Sal. The man's eyes were glazed, and his face was bloodied and bruised.

"Sal, we need to get out of here. That's enough."

He kept going.

Smack. Grunt. Moan.

Blood and saliva splattered everywhere.

I tugged on his suit jacket. "Sal, stop it. Please. Take me home. I want to get out of here before anyone comes."

Scrambling to his feet, he dragged his bloodied hand through his disheveled hair. His gaze cut to me, and a chill rocketed down my spine. Those eyes feathered with shades of green, brown and gold burned into me. Anger radiated out of him like a tidal wave, and my heart stuttered. I'd never seen Sal like this. I didn't know this man. It was like someone had finally pulled back the curtain, and bloodthirst and rage had replaced his mild, caring manner. Even when he shot that man in the warehouse, he'd exercised control and deliberation. He reminded me of a statue or robot. Not today.

"Sal, I-I'm sorry. I should have listened—"

"I don't want to hear it." His hand came down on the back of my neck, both a warning and a gesture of support. Without a word or backward glance he guided me away from the park and toward the street, his stride determined, confident, and filled with authority. The muscles in his jaw jumped and seesawed. People dodged out of his way, their eyes fixed away from him like they feared catching his attention.

I glanced over my shoulder. The man was already on his feet, marching backward, his attention firmly on me. He pointed at me and then at the side of his head reminding me of his message. I stumbled over the uneven pavement when we hit the sidewalk, and Sal's arm slipped around my waist steadying me. I didn't care about his message or the meaning behind it. I only wanted to go home.

A strangled moan worked its way up my constricted throat, stopping before it exited my mouth. I sagged into Sal, wrapping my arms around his waist and tucking me into his side, not caring if he was still angry with me. I needed to be held. I needed something solid to keep my musings out of the quicksand of despair pulling me under with every step closer to his car.

The little freedom and decision-making I had would be over the instant my dad learned what happened tonight. I might as well call him now and tell him to bar my windows and add a keyed lock to my bedroom door. He'd never let me out of his sight, not until he handed me over to Marcello. Then I'd be married and who knew what he'd expect of me?

CHAPTER TWENTY

"How the hell did this happen?"

My father paced back and forth, his leather soles clomping over the floor, repeatedly shoving his hand into his salt and pepper hair. His eyes were darker than normal, and I hadn't been able to find my voice for the last five or ten minutes. I hadn't uttered a single word since we reached my house.

My dad had been waiting, and the minute we stepped over the threshold he unleashed fire and brimstone on Sal. Being a complete and total chicken shit, I did nothing except stare at him. I didn't even correct the inaccuracies he tossed at Sal one after another like grenades.

Sal glanced up, his legs spread and his elbows resting on his knees. "I got there as soon as I parked the car."

"What the fuck were you thinking? Why did you let her walk into the park by herself? You had one job: to accompany my daughter everywhere. And you failed. Angelo said he trusted you. He said next to Gian, you are one of his most reliable guys."

"I'm sorry. It won't happen again." Sal swallowed, his hands curled into fists. "I'll understand if you don't trust me with her anymore."

My father forced out a dry chuckle that had absolutely nothing to do with amusement. "Trust you with my daughter? Hell, right now I don't trust you period. Now get out of my fucking house. I don't want to see your face for at least a week. Angelo can decide what to do with you in the meantime."

"I understand." Sal stood, his broad shoulders squared with defiance, his face a poker mask. I admired his strength, his quiet resistance, and his unwillingness to bend in the face of my father's wrath.

"Wait," I squeaked out, finally finding some modicum of courage beneath the haze of shock. "It wasn't his fault."

My dad leaned over, bracing his hands on the edge of his desk, his black brows flattening. "I didn't ask for your opinion, Emilia. I'll deal with you later in private."

"No." I wiped my hands up and down my legs, doing my best to warm myself from the outside in. "Listen, Dad. I jumped out of the car because Sal refused to let me go to the park alone. I caught him off guard. He came after me as soon as he parked the car. I take full responsibility for what happened."

"Is this true, Sal?" my father asked him.

"It doesn't matter. I should have anticipated her next move. I made a mistake."

"That's not true. It was my fault. I even forgot

124

my phone." I swallowed over the cotton expanding inside my mouth. "And that man, well, he must've been stalking me. He followed me there. He knew my name."

Sal's angry gaze cut to me, and I jerked backward. He'd hardly looked in my direction since we got in his car. It was like he couldn't stand me anymore, and now that I had his attention, I could breathe again. Even with fury blazing from his eyes, my heart filled up under the weight of his attention. I wanted to climb up him like a damn tree and never let go. Somehow over the last six months he'd become my safe space, my anchor, and I had to defend him or my father would squeeze him out of my life. I wouldn't let that happen without a fight.

"What do you mean, he knew you?" My father's icy voice broke Sal's lock on my attention.

"He called me by name and mentioned some man." I tapped my finger on my thigh, trying to recall what he said to me before the shit hit the fan. "Mr. Bonaccorso. That's it. He wanted to make sure you'd honor your arrangement with him."

My dad's face paled, then he picked up his marble pen holder and chucked it. It whirled through the air, crashing against the dark wood paneled wall and shattering when it hit the hardwood floor. The pens and pencils scattered like confetti, rolling to a stop at the edge of the jewel-toned throw rug.

Silence blanketed the room like a thundercloud primed to unleash the full intensity of its fury. My heart thumped in protest as if it could flee the tension in the room and find somewhere to take shelter if it pumped hard enough. I burrowed my fidgeting hands in the hem of my shirt, plucking at the loose threads in a futile effort to mask my growing uneasiness. My father wasn't prone to tantrums. His patented glare, his silent disapproval, and his unspoken power were sufficient to convey his message.

Sal's hands fell on top of my shoulders and I closed my eyes, pretending we were anywhere but here. I played Gershwin's "Rhapsody in Blue" in my head, my fingers tapping softly in time with the invisible notes.

"What else did he say?" my father barked out, pulling me out of the melody dancing inside of my mind.

"Nothing. That's it. Sal showed up a few seconds later and you know what happened after." I cleared my throat. "Who's Mr. Bonaccorso? What does he want? That man said he wouldn't hurt me."

My father's rage evaporated before my eyes like it never existed in the first place. Deadly calm replaced the show of emotion. Staring at me with flat eyes, he adjusted the knot of his silver tie. "Nothing you need to worry about. Sal, I will no longer need you to escort my daughter to piano lessons."

Sal stepped back from me, and I missed his comfort. "Yes, sir. Would you like me to talk to Tony about driving?"

"No." My dad trailed his fingers across the top of his shiny, polished desk. "She won't be taking any lessons. She has too much to do in preparation for her wedding. Her engagement to Marcello will be announced at my Christmas Eve party."

My jaw dropped. "You can't keep me from taking lessons! You know how much they mean to me!"

"You can play the piano upstairs, and once you're married, you can resume your training if your husband agrees. Until then, you cannot leave the house unless accompanied by me. Sal, you'll stay here while I'm not home." His icy gaze sliced to Sal. "Don't fuck this up. You know what's riding on this."

I popped out of my seat like a jack in the box, tears streaming down my face. My hands curled into balls with the urge to lash out at my father. "You can't keep me holed up here like a prisoner! I'm over eighteen. You can't control me anymore. I won't let you. I'm done listening to you. You've taken away everything from me. My music, my future, my dreams, my choices." I hesitated for a fraction of an instant, realizing I was treading into uncharted waters, only I couldn't hold back any longer. "My mom. You're a monster. You drove her to kill herself, and you're doing the same thing to me. Is that what you want?"

My father moved so fast I didn't see it coming. His hand sprang into action, hissing through the air and landing open-palmed against my cheek. Flames spread out from the point of contact, quickly replaced by a throbbing, stinging sensation.

Flabbergasted, I stood in the middle of the room like a moron with my hand cupping the side of my face. A slow burn bubbled in the pit of my stomach that felt a lot like hate, and I zeroed in on that rather than the disillusionment and tears lurking right beneath it. Hate would fuel me. Disillusionment would make me weak.

"Don't talk about things you don't understand, will never understand," my dad growled, his eyes snapping and a cavernous rivet forming between his brows.

The harsh tone of his voice cut through my shock with surgical precision, and all I could think was that I needed to get away from him as fast as possible. My limbs wobbly and my stomach knotting, I staggered out of his office, lumbering up the stairs, blindly seeking the safety of my bedroom. With each step away from the study, my rage built until I was practically foaming at the mouth. When I reached my room, I kicked the door closed, cursing my father for forbidding me from having a lock.

Like a wild animal I whipped my forearm across the top of my dresser. Picture frames, my jewelry box, and hundreds of tiny trinkets spiraled across the surface, colliding with the adjacent wall.

Thud. Crash. Shatter.

The commotion did nothing to improve my mood or rid me of my indignation, so I continued my tirade of destruction. I flung open my drawers one after another, tearing neatly folded clothes from their place, slinging the scraps of fabric across the room. I screamed. I cursed. I cried.

When I emptied my dresser, I stood there glaring at the explosion of mostly black covering the floor, my chest heaving like I'd run for miles. I listened for my father's footsteps, his voice, his anything. Instead, tomblike silence greeted me. My muscles spent and my brain mentally exhausted from expelled rage, I shuffled across the floor to my bed, begging for sleep to take me away from my crappy life for a little while.

CHAPTER TWENTY-ONE

Footsteps echoed in the deathly quiet of my room, and I didn't bother rolling over to see who it was. I didn't care. I couldn't, not when my whole world was coming apart at the seams. The chances of successfully escaping my current life had decreased exponentially. I didn't trust myself to make good on my promise to get away from my dad and the Trassatos regardless of the cost.

"Em, are you awake?"

Oh, God, it was Sal. Still mortified by what he witnessed, I couldn't face him. I squeezed my eyes tighter, willing him to leave me alone, to give me more time to put myself back together.

Either Sal didn't get my message or he chose to ignore it. The bed dipped under his weight, his hip brushing against my knees. He swept my hair away from my face and I mentally cursed the goose bumps popping out on my arms.

"Go away. I don't want to talk to anyone. Ever."

"Come on. It's been almost two weeks. You've showered maybe once, and you've hardly eaten. You're too tiny already. If you aren't careful, you'll waste away into nothing."

"Who cares?" I mumbled.

"I care. I can't stand to see you like this. It's killing me. Christmas Eve is in two days. We have a lot to do."

"Oh, joy. I finally get to meet the man who I'm going to marry. No wait, I mean my new prison warden."

"Hey, a lot of things could happen between now and then. Don't give up."

"Don't give up?" I snarled, flopping onto my back. "That's easy for you to say. You're not the one whose life is in shambles. Don't you get it? My dad has stolen everything from me. My mom, my choice of a husband, and now the last piece of my life that made *me* me—piano."

"So you're going to throw in the towel and let him do this without a fight?"

"I don't see how I have much choice in the matter."

"That's not true. The Emilia I know wouldn't let this happen. You've danced around the fact more than once that you had something up your sleeve. Why don't you tell me what you had in mind? Maybe I can help you."

"I had this plan that I would..." I wimped out mid-sentence, my gaze darting to Sal. Could I trust him? While my heart said yes, my brain said no. I scooted up my headboard and pulled my knees into my chest. "Never mind. It's stupid."

With serious eyes, he studied me for a few beats deliberating something. "I don't think I ever told you this, but I never wanted anything to do with this life. I still don't."

"Wait. I don't get it. Lettie said—"

"Lettie doesn't know shit. She only knows what I want her and everyone else to think. The truth is something entirely different."

Pushing out a nervous huff of laughter, I tugged on the hem of my t-shirt, stretching it over my knees. Participating in a soul-searching session wasn't at the top of my to-do list right now. Mostly because I didn't have the bandwidth mentally or physically. Powerlessness and vulnerability had settled deep in my bones, and I was still freefalling from the fight with my dad.

"Everyone has a private and a public agenda. You're no different from any of the other guys working for my dad. I'd bet ninety percent of them are in it for the power and money rather than the experience of being part of the *family*."

"Can I trust you?" Before I could respond, he swung his legs onto my bed, cozying up beside me. "I already know you're going to tell me I can, but you're wasting your breath. I know you can't make that promise, not with your dad being who he is. Information is a valuable currency in this world, and you could decide to sell me out to get what you want."

I caught his gaze, trying to convey sincerity. "I wouldn't do that."

"I know you wouldn't *want* to do that, but if it came to a choice between you and me, you'd pick yourself every time. I'm not saying you're selfish because you're not. You're desperate. Maybe you're more desperate than me, and that's saying a lot, or maybe it's because my wounds aren't as fresh as yours."

I squinted, puzzling out his cryptic words. "What do you mean?"

"Do you know how Pietro took in my family after my dad died?"

I nodded.

"Well, my mom didn't want to accept his help. I convinced her to move in there, and you know why?"

Not sure I wanted to know, my stomach twisted and turned into tiny knots. "I suppose you needed money."

"Yeah, there was that. Mostly, though, I wanted to find out who killed my dad."

"I heard he was mugged or something."

"That's the official story. I don't believe it."

I frowned. "You don't?"

"No. My dad and Pietro had been butting heads for months. A week before he died, Pietro dropped by our house in the middle of the night. I knew I should've stayed in bed. My dad didn't want me to get sucked into the Family business. He wanted me to go to college as far away from New York as possible and never come back." He paused, his eyes distant like he was reliving something from his past. "Anyway, they were fighting about missing money. My dad threatened to go to Dominick and Angelo if Pietro didn't come clean. He gave him one month to get his shit in order, and my dad was dead a week later. Pietro framed my dad, claiming he stole the money."

My veins iced over. I knew Pietro had something to do with his death. While Lettie had only told me bits and pieces of what went on in her house, it was enough to know that putting a hit on Sal's dad for threatening to rat him out wasn't out of the realm of possibility.

"Holy shit," I wheezed.

"I did the only thing I could think of at the time."

"What's that?"

His eyes latched onto mine again, and for a second he didn't answer. "I ingratiated myself with Pietro, hoping I could prove he killed my dad and took the money."

"Have you found anything?"

"No. Nothing concrete, and I think that's by design. The minute I became a soldier, Dominick assigned me to Angelo rather than Pietro, though I still check in with Pietro here and there and offer to do things for him. That's how we ended up at the warehouse the day we were ambushed."

My breath stalled inside my lungs. "Do you think he had something to do with what happened?"

"I know he did. I just can't prove it yet." He squeezed my leg. "So that's my story. I don't give a shit about the mafia. I wish I were doing anything but being drawn deeper into this world. This life. I had this idea I could get in, vindicate my dad, and get out. Sadly, it doesn't work that way. The only way out of the *family* is death or jail."

"Or the witness protection program," I joked even though it was a real possibility.

"Nah. I'd never do that because as much as I hate Pietro, I love and respect the others. Angelo, Gian, Tony, and even your father in some twisted way because without him, I wouldn't be here with you. You're my reward for all the bad shit even if we can never be more than this, and I'd make the same choices again it if brought me to you. "

You're my reward...

Brought me to you...

His words lodged inside my brain, and if it were possible to glow, I would have. I didn't think he understood how deeply those words affected me. How they simultaneously gutted me and revived me.

He squeezed my thigh. "So are you going to tell me about your plan? You know, now that I just told you all my dirty secrets. Or are you going to leave me hanging?"

I had to tell him. I *wanted* to tell him. And maybe with a little luck, we could be each other's team rather than being alone dealing with our private demons.

"I was trying to dig up enough dirt to threaten my father and force him to let me start a new life somewhere, but I don't think he'll ever let me go. He'll find different ways to control me. The only way out is to leave without a trace, and that's what I'll do when I have enough money to support myself for six months."

"I'll help you."

"No, absolutely not. My father would torture you until you told him where I went, and if that didn't work, he'd flat out kill you. I can't be worried about you while I'm on the run."

He framed my face, directing all of my attention on him. "Then I'll come with you."

A choking noise rolled up my throat, and I couldn't draw a single molecule of air into my lungs. "Oh, Sal..."

"That is, if you want me to go with you."

"You'd do that for me? What about your family and your life here? We could never come back, and you couldn't contact them. Ever."

"You're worth it, Em. Even if you get sick of me and strike out on your own, I wouldn't regret it."

Tears welled in my eyes. No one ever went to bat for me and supported me unconditionally. Normally that was a parent's job. Apparently, my mom and dad never got that memo. My mom loved me in an abstract way. I was something to fill her time between performing and having an active social life. And my dad, well, he only loved me when I did what he wanted.

"C'mere, *tesoro*." He gathered me into his lap, his arms circling my waist. "Don't cry. I didn't mean to come on so strong. You don't have to answer me right now."

"No. No..." I leaned back. "I want you to come with me. I can't believe you'd give up everything for me. Are you sure?"

He pressed his lips against mine and whispered, "Never been so sure of anything in my life."

"What do we do now?"

"We plan."

CHAPTER TWENTY-TWO

Two things happened recently to ensure tonight would be the best Christmas Eve party my father ever had, at least from my perspective. First, Marcello canceled his plans to visit yesterday, claiming he had a family emergency. He rescheduled our engagement announcement for Easter, which was a little over three months away.

I hemmed and hawed, rolled my eyes, and made plenty of snide remarks, not wanting my father to know I didn't give a crap. Sal and I had a plan. We were getting out of here in less than four months. While I wished we could push up our departure so I'd never have to meet Marcello Masciantonio, we wouldn't have enough money by then.

The best part of tonight was the game I came up with. I stashed mistletoe in out of way places all over my house. When everyone reached the tipping point between tipsy and drunk, the game would start, which should be any minute now.

I circled the perimeter of the great room, my shoes clicking over the hardwoods. The traditional Feast of the Seven Fishes for *La Vigilia* was artfully displayed on the large family style table between the kitchen and great room. Stuffed clams, fried anchovies, *baccalà alla vesuviana*, pasta with various shellfish, baked eel, marinated shrimp, and more.

The house smelled like a combination of pine needles from the greenery delivered this morning, garlic, and basil. The alcohol flowed freely from an impromptu bar set up near the precast fireplace manned by Tony in his Santa suit.

My brain was foggy from indulging in more than one glass of Prosecco, and I couldn't reverse the smile on my face if I tried, not that anyone noticed me. They were wrapped up in their conversations, the chatter going from a hum to a roar spiked with laughter in the last twenty minutes.

Sal had a tumbler of whiskey in one hand and his other arm around Gian's shoulder. Nearly the same age, it was natural for them to be friends. And as much as I rebelled against everything to do with my family, I didn't dislike Carmela or Gian. Truthfully, I was so dead set on wallowing in my misery, I never gave them much of a chance, and now that I was leaving, having a relationship with them would never happen.

When I snagged Sal's gaze, I lifted my champagne glass to my lips and tipped my head to the side. The light bubbles fizzled on my tongue all the way down my throat to my belly, mixing with the jumpiness already tumbling around in there.

Sal shot me a cocky grin, then dropped his arm from Gian's shoulder. Without waiting to see if he followed, I placed my empty glass on a nearby end table and made my way through the kitchen to the mudroom, closing the pocket door behind me. A tiny sprig of glossy green leaves with a burst of red berries dangled from the domed polished nickel light fixture.

I stood directly beneath it, waiting for Sal to join me. Minutes ticked by, and my nerves stretched thin. I started pacing. Did he get caught? Waylaid? Change his mind?

The roar of laughter and clinking glasses floated into the room. I leaned against the white cabinets, defeat coiling around my chest. Maybe it was better if he stayed away. If someone caught us, my dad would summon Marcello to marry me by the New Year, and Sal, well, my dad would destroy him.

Seeing the stupidity of my game, I slid open the door determined to do the right thing and to rejoin the party, only I didn't get far. Sal stood at the threshold, one side of his mouth hitched upward in knowing grin.

"You're already giving up on me? I got accosted by your dad."

He moved forward and like a choreographed dance I edged back. The soft thud of the closing door echoed in the small space. I pressed my hand to the center of my chest to calm my racing heart.

"No, just rethinking the wisdom of meeting you like this. I mean, if someone saw us—"

"Shh." He pressed two fingers to my mouth, cutting me off. "Nobody will be looking for us, and you've been driving me crazy since I walked in the door."

"Me?"

"Yes, you. Alessandro has been following you around all night like a puppy. If it weren't so damn pathetic, I would punch him in the face. Did anything ever happen between you two?"

Alessandro was Pietro's son and Lettie's stepson. While he had been hanging around me tonight more than usual, he wasn't interested in me, or at least I didn't think so. I never gave him reason to believe I liked him as more than a friend. We were nearly the same age, and we used to go to school together until my dad pulled me out in favor of homeschooling. As far as I was concerned, that was it.

"You're being ridiculous. I'm not interested in him as more than a friend."

He pursed his lips in annoyance. "I don't think he got that message."

"I don't agree. He's not interested in me, so stop being a jealous jerk."

His now angry eyes held me captive. "I'm not jealous. I'm protective."

"Is that right?"

"I don't want to talk about him," he pointed to the ceiling, "when there's mistletoe demanding I do my duty."

I arched an eyebrow, my lips twitching. "Your duty, huh? Maybe I changed my mind."

"Oh, no you don't." He closed the space between us, pressing me into cabinets adjacent to the garage door. He joined our hands together, resting them against the polished black countertop. "I came here to kiss a beautiful woman, my woman, beneath the mistletoe and wish her a Merry Christmas." His lips brushed across mine gently. "And with any luck, next year we'll be in a place where we can celebrate in the open. Without your father or that little shit, Alessandro."

He kissed me, and I felt it all the way down to the tips of my toes and up to the roots of my hair. I yanked one of my hands from his grip, and my fingertips traced his jawline, down his neck and rested my palm against the firm plane of his chest over his thudding heart. His free hand painted a line up my thigh, snaking under my skirt, cupping my ass. The tips of his fingers gripped me tightly, claiming me as his own and God, did I wish he could. A moan tumbled from my mouth. I wanted to tell him I loved him and so many other things that had been swirling around in my mind over the last two days.

I twirled his red tie around my wrist, kissing him like it had been years and not mere days since my lips touched his.

"I wish we could run away tomorrow. I don't want to wait four more months," he muttered.

A tremor rippled through me. "Me neither…" I mumbled, wanting to drag him out the garage door and steal away before anyone noticed. My errant thoughts faded from my mind when his lips moved down my neck. My body burst to life with every caress, kiss, and puff of air.

He lifted me on to the top of the counter, wedging his legs between mine, and kept kissing me, drinking me in until I was boneless and limp, wondering how I'd find the energy to get off this counter and rejoin the party. Even worse, I was certain my cheeks were flushed and my hair frazzled, but I set out to boycott all my worries of the future tonight, and that was precisely what I intended to do right now.

Glass shattered outside the door, and he broke the kiss, chuckling. "Well someone has piss poor timing." He pulled me off the counter and handed me the broom from the closet. "Take this in there, and I'll slip out the garage service door, smoke a cigar before coming back inside."

My throat dry, and my hands still unsteady, I nodded as he opened the door.

"Em," he said, pushing a strand of hair behind my ear, "I'll come find you in an hour at the next meeting spot. The sunroom right?"

"Yeah," I whispered, watching the garage door close behind him, my heart drunk on love and his skillful kisses.

With a broom clutched in my hand, I rolled open the door. Only Alessandro and Lettie were nearby. Lettie was leaning against the refrigerator with her arms folded across her chest, glaring. Alessandro stood directly across from her, his shoulder braced against the wall with a smirk on his face. Remnants of a broken champagne glass and bubbly liquid coated the floor between them.

CHAPTER TWENTY-THREE

"What happened?" I asked, my gaze ping-ponging between the two of them.

"Yeah, Lettie." Alessandro kicked a sliver of glass away from his boot-clad feet. "Why don't you explain how your drink ended up in my face?"

Lettie straightened her shoulders and flipped her long dark hair over her shoulder. "Fuck you."

"Nah," he chuckled. "Thanks for the offer, but I'm not a big fan of sloppy seconds, or in your case sloppy hundreds. Too bad my dad doesn't have the same standards."

Red streaks shot up Lettie's face and she balled her hands into fists next to her thighs. "I hate you."

He pressed a hand to his chest. "Say it isn't so. What will I do without your love?"

"I'm done with this conversation." Not meeting my eyes, she stormed out of the kitchen, her four-inch heels exploding like bombs against the hardwood floor, and the fabric of her body-hugging emerald green velvet dress pulling taut with every step.

"Of course you are!" he yelled after her.

I dragged the broom over the floor, waiting for Alessandro to explain. When he didn't say anything, I asked, "So are you going to tell me what that was about?"

He got the dustpan from the mudroom, snatched the broom from my hand, and finished cleaning the mess without answering.

"I guess not," I said, frustrated with him and Lettie. "So much for us being friends."

"Jesus, Emilia." He ran his fingers through his sandy brown hair. "Do you really want to talk about this here?"

"Talk about what?"

He pointed a finger at me, his lips thin and his color high. "I don't know what you were thinking, but you need to be more discreet."

"I think you got the two of us confused. I'm not the one who had a full glass of champagne tossed in my face."

He stalked across the kitchen and tilted up my chin with the tip of his finger, his soft brown eyes full of fire. "I don't know what the fuck is going on between you and Sal." I opened my mouth to fire off a sarcastic retort, and he glared in warning. "No, I don't want to know. The less I know the better, because whatever shit happened in the mudroom needs to end."

I slapped his hand away from my face, anger and humiliation curling inside my gut. "It's none of your business. Stay out of it."

"Emilia, I'm only saying this to you because I like you, and you don't deserve half the shit your dad does to you, but you and Sal cannot happen. Period. End of story. Your father would kill you if he found out, especially now that he has set up some arrangement with the Masciantonios. And fuck, Sal is already treading on thin ice. My dad only partially trusts him, and if he found you two have been doing whatever, he'd be in *your* dad's office arguing to do the honors of fitting Sal for a pair of cement boots and sending him on a long swim in the Hudson."

My heart skipped a beat, and I blurted out the first lie that popped into my brain. "Sal and I were talking. That's it. I promise. We should have left the door open. I wasn't thinking clearly."

"Bullshit." He slanted into me, eliminating any suggestion of space. "I saw you. So did Lettie. She was spying on you, and that bitch is not right in the head. I'd watch your back from now on. I know you've got it in your head that she's your friend, but let me clue you in—Lettie is no one's friend except her own. She is a sociopath."

My stomach flipped, and bile inched its way up my throat. My mind scrambled to wrap itself around his words. "What do you mean she was spying on us?"

"She followed Sal in here, and I caught her peeking through the gap in the doorway. That's why she tossed the glass at me. I told her to mind her own fucking business and get a life."

"Oh shit," I whispered.

"Oh shit is right."

I dug my fingers into the hem of his suit jacket. "What should I do? Do you think she's talking to my dad right now? I need to find Sal and tell him what's—"

"No." He glanced over his shoulder. "She's more calculating than that. She'll wait until she can use it to her advantage."

"Why do you think she followed me?"

"Who knows? She's weird about Sal, though."

"Why? Were they…" I couldn't bring myself to finish the sentence. The image of Sal doing anything with Lettie made my stomach lurch. He'd warned me away from her more than once, and I wondered if it had more to do with keeping a secret than her being a bad friend.

He shrugged. "Who knows? Lettie's like a spider, luring people into her web. Maybe she got to Sal at some point."

The glow from being with Sal had dimmed, and all the happiness inside of me following his promise to leave with me shriveled up and died. I felt lost. Alone. Confused. Like I'd lost my favorite possession.

"Hey." Alessandro squeezed my upper arms and pressed a kiss to each of my cheeks, snapping me out of my fog. "Don't look so sad. I've never seen them do anything other than talk. If anything, Sal was colder to her than I ever was when he lived with us. He barely acknowledged her presence. I'm just throwin' theories out there for why she's so interested in the two of you."

Air whooshed out of my lungs and I nodded, feeling marginally better. "Yeah. Who knows?" I cleared my throat to wash away the sour taste in my mouth. "Thanks for the warning. I'm going to say goodbye to everyone and go to bed. I think I'm done for the night."

He stepped back, releasing me from his hold. "That's probably a good idea."

"When do you head back to school?"

"Not for a couple of weeks, but I'm leaving my dad's house the day after Christmas."

"Where are you headed?"

"To LA. I'm meeting up with some friends for the New Year, so I won't see you again for a while. You know I go to extremes to avoid everything to do with my father."

"Must be nice to have so much freedom."

His eyes darkened, and his lips curved downward. "Don't be fooled. We all have baggage, and trust me, the grass isn't always greener."

"Isn't that the truth? Enjoy the rest of your break." I took a couple of steps. "Oh, and have Happy New Year, Sandro."

"You too, Emilia."

CHAPTER TWENTY-FOUR

The possibility something had happened between Sal and Lettie gnawed at my gut long after Sandro dropped that bomb on me. For the next hour, I studied Sal and Lettie's behavior, looking for hints of the truth. Sadly, my efforts failed to shed light on anything. Sal didn't once glance in Lettie's direction, and Lettie's husband made sure she didn't leave his side.

Apparently old habits die hard, because part of me pitied her when I saw his fingers dig into Lettie's hip or anger flash across his face. She'd done something to piss him off, which wasn't all that usual. As far as I could tell, nothing she did seemed to please him. I had no clue why he'd married her, or stayed married for that matter. Maybe it was about control.

Unlike in the past, I didn't approach them and attempt to relieve the tension. She'd suffer when they returned to the privacy of their house. I had no desire to come to her aid tonight, though. That probably made me a terrible person, and I couldn't find it in my heart to care. All of our shared confidences and laughs took on a sinister bent. Lettie had her own agenda, one that included stepping all over me if it helped her, and I'd never trust her again.

Ten minutes before Sal and I were supposed to meet at the next pre-arranged mistletoe location, he caught my eye. Frowning, he cocked his head and pointed to the front entryway. I shook my head and went back to the kitchen where I could slip up the service stairs and into my bedroom without calling attention to my absence. I needed to get my thoughts in order before I talked to him and that meant spending some time alone.

Instead of finding clarity in the privacy of my room, I found another black and white wrapped present from Marcello sitting on my desk. He hadn't sent me anything except a note or two since the bracelet. My heart sped up as I peeled off the wrapping paper. I found a framed black and white headshot of my mom inside. In the lower right-hand corner, she had written:

"All my love, Ava Accorso."

Marcello had taped another note to the back of the frame. Part of me wanted to ignore it or dump it in the trash. With my dream of Sal and me riding off into the sunset hanging by a thread, I didn't know if I could handle any more unsettling news tonight. I unlocked my top desk drawer, kicking around the idea of saving it for another day.

Fuck it.

I unfolded it. If anything, the letter would take my mind off Sal and Lettie.

Emilia,

I came across this picture last month, and I wanted to give it to you in person. Unfortunately, my sister had an accident, and I had to stick around to help her despite all her protests that she'd be fine alone. It's probably better this way. I could only stay in New York for a couple of days because of business commitments. I'll have more free time in spring.

Merry Christmas,

Marcello.

P.S. I heard your family calls you the dark fairy. Should I be worried? When I was a kid someone told the story of the Orculli who are cannibalistic fairies that live in the clouds of Italy and eat unsuspecting humans.

Laughing, I pulled out a piece of paper to respond.

Marcello,

My mom told me the story of the Orculli, and I can safely say you won't confuse me with them. I'm pretty sure the Orculli are male, bearded, fae giants who smell like rotting carcasses. At a little over five feet, I could hardly be confused for a giant, and I assure you that I don't have anything resembling a beard on my face. As for my smell, while nobody has complained, people can be cruel backstabbing jerks so who knows?

Wait! Upon further reflection, I've decided to confess I'm half Orculli, complete with a beard and cannibalistic tendencies. The smell gene hasn't presented itself though, so you won't have to hold your nose when we're in the same room, but I've heard that might change with age kind of like cheese.

XO

Emilia, the half Orculli

P.S. I eagerly await your immediate rejection of our engagement/marriage.

I fell asleep that night with a smile on my face thinking of my ridiculous response. A week went by before I received another letter from him.

Emilia the half Orculli,

Have you heard of laser hair removal? I'm sure we can do something to get rid of your excess hair, and I've seen that picture of your mom, so I'm sure I'll be happy with what's underneath. As for the cannibalistic tendencies, I'm not opposed to a few love bites as long as you don't draw blood. I'm positive we can come up with a compromise. I've been told I'm a good problem solver.

Marcello the Wise

I waited five days to reply to him. I didn't want him to think I liked exchanging letters with him.

Marcello the Wise,

What kind of compromise were you considering? I'm not into human sacrifice. It's messy, so I do my best to restrict my diet to animals and other fairies these days. It's not always easy, and sometimes I can't help myself. You should keep your distance if you want to stay safe. I think Chicago and New York are far enough apart, so rest assured, you will remain intact as long as you don't seek me out.

Emilia the Bloodthirsty

Three days later came his answer.

Emilia the Bloodthirsty,

Would you agree to wear a muzzle when you have the urge to eat something other than animals or fairies? By the way, where does one find a fairy to offer up to a half-Occulli these days? I stumbled on an article on making a fairy trap. Perhaps I should investigate this so I have one ready when we meet in a couple of months. I'd hate for our relationship to end before its starts because you were hungry.

Marcello the Fairy Trapping Apprentice

CHAPTER TWENTY-FIVE

Sal flung open my bedroom door without knocking. "When are you going to stop ignoring me?"

Not answering him for a second, I reread my last letter to Marcello.

Marcello the Fairy Trapping Apprentice,

No need to expend any effort trapping a fairy. In all honesty, I hate winged creatures. All of them. Birds, bugs, bats, butterflies. Even fairies. (I don't have wings so I'm not self-hating.) They all give me the creeps so you'll have to come up with a different title for yourself.

Emilia the Wing Hater

I had no clue why I continued to write Marcello. No, that wasn't entirely true. I hated to admit it, but I kind of liked having somebody to talk to that wasn't in my everyday life. Sometime over the last month, he'd stopped being the enemy and turned into a confidant of sorts. Maybe even a friend, and if he were my friend, he might agree to let me go. We'd part ways without any hard feelings, and my dad couldn't do a damn thing about it.

"I've been busy." I stuffed the letter into the top drawer of my desk and faced him. "I haven't been ignoring you."

"Come on, Emilia. Don't play games with me." Sal shifted his hip, leaning against my doorframe. "You blew me off on Christmas Eve, and you haven't said more than hello and goodbye to me in nearly a month. Did you dump me without bothering to tell me?"

Staring blankly at the wall above his head, I struggled to put my feelings into words. He was right. I had been avoiding him. Truthfully, I couldn't get the conversation with Alessandro out of my head. His words were tattooed in my brain. While his accusation wasn't enough to talk me out of wanting Sal, it hung over me, taunting me with the possibility of it being the truth.

As badly as I wanted to ask Sal about his history with Lettie, I hadn't found the courage to do it. If he confessed to having some sort of relationship with her, I didn't know if I could get past it. I hated the thought of her having a claim on Sal, no matter how insignificant.

Even worse, I needed to tell Sal Lettie and Alessandro saw us, and that would bring up a whole other set of issues. Deep in my gut, I dreaded the possibility Sal would flake on me, and I'd be on my own again, spinning my wheels, struggling to break free.

"Don't exaggerate. I've talked to you. I even kissed you goodnight last week." I drew one of my knees into my chest and wrapped my arms around it. "And my father's been around a lot lately so it's not as if we've had many opportunities to hang out or anything. It's like he senses I'm going to take off and he's watching me like a hawk."

He crossed the room and sat on the edge of my bed. "Kisses on the cheek don't count, but your dad's gone all day today so you can kiss me all you want. I won't complain."

I swallowed, my throat suddenly dry at the prospect of being around Sal uninterrupted for hours on end. He wouldn't let me hide from him today without an explanation.

"So he said. Who knows, though? My dad could pop in here any second. You know how he is."

"Did I push you too hard? Is that what this is about?"

I glanced at him quickly, then returned my attention to the tips of my gray painted toenails. "I've already told you I'm fine with what happened between us."

"Fine with it." He chuckled quietly. "Now that's a ringing endorsement if I've ever heard one. Just so you know, my ego took a huge nosedive and it might never recover."

"Whatever." I rolled my eyes, unsuccessfully fighting the urge to smile. "You didn't push me into anything I didn't want. In fact, it's probably the other way around. You're always saying no, and I'm always trying to change your mind. I think our roles have reversed."

"I knew my sarcastic girl was still in there somewhere." Wrapping his foot around the leg of my chair, he scooted me close enough that his breath grazed the side of my face. "Now are you going to tell me what's going on in that head of yours or do I have to pry it out of you piece by piece?"

"There's nothing to tell."

"Uh huh." He lifted me, tossing me flat on my back on my bed. Bracing his hands next to my shoulders, he rolled partially on top of me. "What's your preferred method of torture today? Kissing or tickling?"

"You wouldn't."

"Oh, I would." His hand shifted to my neck, making its way to my armpit, pausing there for a second. "Decide."

"Neither." I grabbed his wrist, attempting to hold him in place.

"Five. Four. Three."

"Don't you dare."

His smile widened. "Two. One. Too late," he announced as his hand dove in, tickling me until I couldn't breathe and my body was wiggling like a lunatic.

"Stop. Stop! I'll tell you. Please. I'm going to

pee my pants!" I said between ragged pants.

"Okay." His hands curled around my waist. "Go ahead. Spill."

"Ugh. You jerk," I said without heat.

He flexed his hand, silently threatening to continue tickling. "Go on."

"All right." I kept my gaze planted over his shoulder. "Did you ever..." My heart picked up speed.

"Say what you need to say. I'm not going be mad at you."

"Were you and Lettie ever together? You know, intimate?"

His eyes narrowed, all humor melting from his face. "Where the hell did that come from?"

"Alessandro said something after I left the mudroom that made me think you and Lettie hooked up in the past."

"Fucking Alessandro. I really hate that guy."

"So it is true?" My voice quivered on the last syllable.

"There's nothing going on between Lettie and me. I don't like her. I already told you that."

"You promise?" I searched his face for any signs he wasn't telling the truth. I didn't see anything except anger.

"Lettie's married."

"So?"

"I already told you how I thought Pietro had something to do with my dad's death. Why would I get tangled up with his wife?"

"To get even."

"He doesn't give a shit about his wife. She's a

trophy on his arm, that's all. He's still with Alessandro's mom."

My eyes widened. "What?"

"Shit. I shouldn't have said anything. Look, don't tell Lettie. I'm pretty sure she knows, but I don't think she wants it known, if you understand what I mean."

"If Pietro is still with his ex, why'd he marry Lettie?"

"Because his ex's parents threatened to disown her if she kept Alessandro or married Pietro. She married someone else ten years ago, but apparently she refuses to give up Pietro or he won't let her. Who knows? And frankly, I don't give a shit either way. The whole family is twisted as fuck, including Alessandro."

"Yeah, you're probably right."

He framed my face with his hands, his eyes searching mine. "I am right. Now are you going to stop ignoring me? Because I can't do this anymore, Em. I miss you. You haven't touched me in a month. It's killing me."

"I'm sorry. I miss you too." I slid my hand around his nape and pulled his lips against mine. My reservations about him, about us, ceased to exist, along with my conflicted feelings for Marcello.

"So much, Sal."

"Don't do that again." He shifted onto his elbows, breaking our kiss. "Promise me you'll talk to me when you're worried about something instead of bottling it all up."

"I promise."

"Good, because you're the only one I want. Will ever want." His body melded into mine and he kissed me everywhere—my lips, my cheeks, my forehead, my eyelids, and I was lost in him.

CHAPTER TWENTY-SIX

The last few months were filled with a flurry of preparations and so much love. It was true. I loved Sal so freakin' much. I'd been dying to tell him those three magic words for the last months, and I would soon because I couldn't imagine my life without him, his kisses, and his heated touches. The way he looked at me when he didn't think I was watching made my heart swell twenty times its size, and for the first time in my life, I felt full rather than half empty.

Footsteps echoed outside of my closed door, and I stuffed the clutch wallet filled with fifteen thousand dollars into my duffle bag and slid it to the back of my closet behind the rows of neatly hung pants. Only two weeks until Easter, and Sal and I had everything we needed to vanish without a trace. Money; clothes; bus tickets; a route; a plan.

Love.

My door hinges squeaked, and I whirled around,

my hand pressed to my chest.

"Did I scare you?" Sal said, closing the door behind him.

"Yes. Jesus. I was going through my getaway bag again, and I thought you were my dad."

He crossed the room and lifted me into his arms, spinning me into a circle. "Stop digging in there. Everything's ready to go, and you *are* going to get caught one of these days if you keep double checking it."

"I know, I know. I can't believe it's all coming together, though, and I have this weird compulsion to make sure the money hasn't disappeared."

"I have something for you that might alter our plans." He pulled an envelope out of the pocket inside his navy suit jacket and handed it to me.

"What's this?" I grabbed it, twirled it around in my hands, then opened it. Inside was a business card from the Royal Conservatory in London. Hope rushed up from my stomach like a balloon. "What's this for?"

"Your dad told me your piano teacher had some things of yours and he asked me to swing by and pick them up. I was expecting books or a lost jacket. She handed me that envelope asking that you contact Darryl Wright. Apparently, he's holding a place for you this fall."

"What's the catch?"

"You have to show up sometime before June for an in-person interview, but according to Mrs. Vitali it's nothing more than a formality. There's a place there if you want it."

"I can't believe it. It's too good to be true." I

stepped back until my legs hit the bed, and I plopped down on top of the mattress.

"I know." He took a seat next to me. "This is perfect, right? We can fly to London or somewhere else in Europe and explore for a week or two before heading to the conservatory. Or we can skip the conservatory altogether. My *nonna* lives outside of Napoli, and I haven't seen her in a decade. She's too old to travel to the U.S. by herself. She wouldn't mind if we stayed with her for a while."

"God, I'd love that. I've never been out of the tristate area, much less out of the country."

"Neither have I."

"Don't you think my father will look for me at music conservatories? I mean, we fought about it for days, and I stopped talking to him after he refused to let me go. It'd be one of the first places he'd look. And crap, we'll need passports, which means I'll need to leave the house at some point. He hasn't let me go anywhere in weeks." My shoulders sagged. "This sucks."

"Don't worry about it. I have a contact that can get both of us a passport with new identities."

"Won't my father find out?"

"No. He doesn't know this guy. He's someone I met a couple of years ago."

"Speaking of my dad, where is he today?"

My father left the house less and less these days. Either he suspected I was up to something or he was so close to his goal of marrying me off to Marcello and he didn't want anything to go wrong at the last minute.

"He had some stuff to take care of. He'll be back

in time for dinner."

Nodding, I stuffed the business card into my back pocket. "So we have three or so hours."

"Yeah, but we can't go anywhere."

I rolled my eyes and climbed onto his lap, straddling him. "Of course. I wouldn't expect anything else. Not with how irrational my father is these days. You'd think there was a serial killer on the loose intent on hauling me off to his personal torture chamber before dismembering me piece by piece."

"Hmm." Sal glanced to the side, breaking eye contact.

"What is it?" I guided his face back to me so he couldn't look away.

"It's probably nothing."

"No. You're not hiding information from me. I've had enough of that with my dad. He's got it in his head that he can protect me by keeping the truth from me and I hate it. It makes me feel like a brainless child who can't put two thoughts together."

"It's nothing, Em. Really. Trust me on this. And none of this will matter because we'll be gone in a month anyway."

I pushed him onto his back. "Tell me."

"I'd rather kiss you."

"You can do both." I toyed with the top button of his sky blue collared shirt for a few beats before popping it open. I repeated the process until I reached the bottom. I traced the grooves of his hard chest down to his abdomen. His muscles bunched and jumped beneath my fingertips, and his Adam's apple bobbed in his neck.

"Stop. We can't do this."

Smirking, I tugged on his belt buckle, loosening it. "Why? You don't want me to touch you?"

"Dammit." His hand clamped around my wrist. "It isn't a matter of want, Em. You know that. We've had this discussion a hundred times. I'm not going to do anything else with you until you're mine."

I pressed a kiss to the corner of his mouth, rocking back and forth so I could feel every inch of him. "I am yours. I've been yours for almost a year now, and it pisses me off that you're still holding back. You haven't done anything except kiss me since that time in your apartment. Are you sick of me?"

Groaning, he squeezed his eyes closed for a second, and released my hand. "I'm trying to be the good guy here and protect you. There are things you don't know. Things you don't need to know. Just know that I have your best interest in mind and every choice I make is for you. You're all that matters. Don't ever forget that."

My heart melted into a pile of mush, and undoubtedly my face was beaming like a light bulb. I loved this guy so much, and while he may not have told me, I could tell he felt the same way. I was so lucky to have found Sal. I may have a shitty father who planned to pawn me off on some random guy, but I won the lottery with Sal.

"You don't need to protect me." I peppered kisses over his neck and chest, getting high on his salty taste and masculine scent. "In less than a

166

month we'll be far away from here. There's nothing to worry about now. Everything is set. We'll either get lost in some mountain town or we'll go to Italy. There's nothing preventing us from being together. We don't have to wait."

Even as I muttered the words, I knew they were a lie. There were plenty of things to worry about. Marcello Masciantonio was a wildcard. He could force me to go to Chicago with him when he left. He could read more into our letters than I intended. My father could make Sal disappear if he found out about us.

And I couldn't forget Lettie. I'd cut her out of my life and refused all of her phone calls. I couldn't face her after she spied on Sal and me. While I hoped she'd drop out of my life without forcing a confrontation, it didn't look like I'd be that lucky. She showed up unannounced last week, and I told my father to send her away because I didn't feel well. He didn't question me even though he knew I was lying, and I was grateful. Five minutes after he sent her home, she fired off a text warning me not to push her out of my life along with a bunch of other cryptic stuff about not knowing the real Sal. I didn't respond. I had absolutely nothing to say to her. She showed her true colors, and I no longer wanted her anywhere near me.

Sal's hands slipped under the hem of my shirt, bracketing my ribcage, and he ran his mouth up the side of my neck. Goose bumps sprinkled my arms.

"Don't kid yourself. So much could still go wrong, and I won't have it on my conscience that I took your virginity and you were forced to marry

Marcello. He'd make your life hell."

"He won't even notice." I infused my words with more conviction than I felt. I didn't know crap about Marcello except for the little hints of his humor I saw in his letters. Even thinking about them made me smile. Each one bolstered my opinion that we could be friends.

"He would."

"Why does it matter? It's not the eighteen hundreds, and I seriously doubt he saved himself for me. If I end up with him because of some weird twist of fate, I'd be happier knowing I gave my virginity to you, someone I care about, rather than a stranger who married me to cement an alliance with my father. So you see, regardless of the how this turns out, I want to be with you. I want you to be my first."

He picked me up and set me on the bed, leaving at least a foot of space between us. "I can't. Not yet. Trust me, okay? I know things you don't."

"What do you know?"

He rubbed the back of his neck, his shoulders tense and his brow scrunched together. "Things about Marcello. Your dad made promises to him and…let's just wait like we planned. Look at it as a celebration of finally being free from all this."

My shoulders sagged. Sal wouldn't cave. I'd pushed him too many times to count, and he never budged from his talking points. He had the patience of a saint. I'd never even had sex, and I lived in a state of perpetual frustration.

"Fine. You win," I grumbled.

"It will be so much better this way, and I can

wait."

"It's torture."

"No shit. Kissing you, having your body pressed against mine, knowing we can't do anything…" His sinful lips pulled upward. "Well, maybe we can kiss a few more times. You know, so we can catch up for those weeks you ignored me after Christmas."

"That sounds fair."

He pulled me into an intoxicating kiss, erasing any lingering feelings of rejection from my mind. He was talented like that.

CHAPTER TWENTY-SEVEN

I ran my brush through my hair one more time, studying my reflection in the mirror. My lips were painted a soft pink. I had blackened my already dark eyelashes with mascara, and they resembled butterfly wings. My wavy hair looked like black silk against the strapless lavender lace dress hugging my slight curves. The woman staring back at me bore no resemblance to the real me, which in some respects was fitting given the deception I was about to commit.

Marcello Masciantonio was waiting downstairs to be formally introduced to me for the first time, believing we were on our way to being married. That would never happen. I couldn't let it happen.

A knock sounded at the door, and I pushed out a ragged breath. God, I didn't want to do this. My heart clutched tightly at the notion of going downstairs and putting on a show for my family and my father's acquaintances. I'd smile, I'd laugh, and a man I had never seen except one time years ago would announce our engagement.

"Come in." My voice was strained, and my stomach was rolling with vinegar.

The thud of footsteps echoed in my room, and I lifted my gaze, latching onto my father's reflection in the mirror. A smile stretched across his normally stoic face making him appear ten years younger.

I spun around, taking in his dark, crisp suit. Today he had on a mint green tie with light blue stripes instead of his usual red or black, probably a nod to it being Easter.

"You look so much like your mother. She'd be so proud of you."

"Thank you," I mumbled, not wanting to talk about my mother. She wouldn't be proud of my father or me tonight. While she may have been preoccupied with her love of music, she always stressed the idea of finding the right person to marry. According to her, life was so much easier when you married a partner, not an adversary. Despite our letters, I didn't have any illusions that Marcello would be anything other than an adversary. We wanted different things, different lives. Sal, on the other hand, had shown me time and time again that we were on the same wavelength, and most importantly, he didn't want anything to do with the mafia.

"I have something for you." My dad pulled a rectangular box from inside his jacket and opened it. Inside was a long strand of gray pearls with a diamond-encrusted clasp. Even though I hadn't seen this piece for years, I recognized it immediately. "I gave them to your mother as an engagement gift. She would want you to have them."

Tears threatened to leak down my face, and I blinked them back, stifling the emotion. "They're beautiful. She used to wear them all the time when I was little." I couldn't count the number of times I watched her rotate her fingers over the pearls absentmindedly. She wore them nearly every day until the fighting with my dad started.

"May I?" He dangled the strand from two fingertips. Nodding, I turned my back to him and lifted my hair. He fiddled with the clasp, then the cold strand hit the back of my neck, and I shuddered.

"I bought them for your mom because they matched her eyes."

I turned to face him. "She never told me that."

"I don't think she knew." He slid his arm through mine. "We should go. I wanted to give you a few moments with Marcello before everyone gets here."

"Okay. That's probably a good idea." I trod down the stairs on my dad's arm, my mouth dry and my legs like jelly.

This is irrelevant.

None of this matters.

I'll be gone in less than a month.

My dad pushed open the heavy walnut and glass door to his study, and the sound of the door latch boomed like a gunshot in my ears. Unable to move, I froze in my tracks.

"It'll be okay. You have nothing to worry about. You'll see."

My father guided me forward, and I fixed my eyes on the profile of a man dressed in a crisp navy suit with a pale lavender tie and a starched white shirt. Apparently, my dad told him the color of my dress so we could match. On any other man the lavender tie might look effeminate, but somehow he succeeded in looking even more masculine.

He had one elbow propped on the precast mantle and a lowball of amber liquid in one hand. He had a Roman nose, long with a high bridge. His inky hair contrasted with his olive skin, and even years later I recognized him as the man arguing with my dad in the study a lifetime ago.

"Marcello, I would like to present my daughter, Emilia Trassato." He released my arm and nudged me forward.

His head whipped toward me, his stare wintry and implacable. His face was lean and harsh with dimple-like grooves framing his mouth. He looked dangerous in a way that both drew me to him and repelled me. I searched for traces of the man who wrote those letters to me, and I didn't see anything except ruthlessness and determination. A chill raced between my shoulder blades, and for a fraction of a second I contemplated turning around and running away from him, this party, and my life.

Without him even opening his mouth, I already gathered that he wasn't someone you screwed over, and I'd been actively plotting to do that for years. There'd be hell to pay when I left in a month's time. I almost felt bad that my father would have to deal with the consequences alone. Then I remembered this quagmire was his own creation, and I felt a considerably better.

"Miss Trassato, it's a pleasure to see you." His voice was smoky, and his lips verged on mocking as they curved into a partial grin. He crossed the room with quick, deliberate strides and pressed an impersonal kiss to each of my cheeks. My heart sped up both from the brief contact and from the trepidation coiling around my lungs.

"Hello, Mr. Masciantonio." I sounded as if I ate sandpaper for breakfast.

My father glanced at his watch. "Everyone will start arriving in fifteen minutes. I'll come in and get you both then, and we'll make the announcement."

"Give us closer to a half an hour," Marcello said, his voice brooking no argument. "We have a lot of things to discuss before we make an announcement."

"Everything is already settled," my father shot back.

Marcello shrugged. "It's not a big deal. I'd like to make sure your daughter and I are on the same page. That's all."

My father turned the force of his attention on me, his eyes communicating silent threats not to mess this up, or maybe it was my imagination. "I'll be back soon."

When the door closed behind him, I flinched, and my heart ground to a momentary halt.

"Let's sit." Marcello waved a hand in the direction of the camel leather sofa.

"I'll stand."

He chuckled and grabbed my hand. When I tried to pull it away he tightened his grip. "I'm not your enemy, Emilia, but that will change if you fight me."

"Why are you doing this?" I asked, hoping to appeal to the man from the letters, not this cold, hard person in front of me. Surely, *that* man would free both of us from this barbaric bargain.

He cocked his head to the side, one inky brow arched and his startling blue eyes skewering me. "This?"

"Agreeing to marry me? I'm sure there are plenty of women in Chicago that'd be happy to have you. I don't understand what would possess you to marry someone you've never seen."

He released my hand and lifted his glass to his lips, drinking the last sip and setting it onto a side table. "I've seen you. Or have you already forgotten that I caught you spying on my conversation with your father years ago?"

"That doesn't count."

"I've seen you since then."

When?"

"I watched a piano performance about six months ago. I think it was your last one."

"Why didn't you approach me?"

"You were otherwise engaged."

"Otherwise engaged? You mean performing?"

"No. I came backstage afterward."

"Oh, right. Someone approached me about studying at a music conservatory. I guess I was preoccupied that night."

He smiled, but nothing about it was friendly. "I heard about that. I was talking about the man kissing you though."

My entire body froze, and I struggled to draw enough air into my constricted lungs. "I think you're mistaken."

"Am I?"

My attention bounced around the room looking at anything other than him. Fessing up would probably be the best course of action right now. It'd smooth things over, earn me some honesty points, and in the long run it wouldn't matter since I was never going to marry him. Something inside of me blocked the confession from surfacing, and I settled on a whitewashed version of the truth.

"Hmm. Maybe you're right. I can't remember that night all too well. I was excited about a scholarship offer, and it's entirely possible I kissed someone in celebration. You know, now that I think about it that's probably what you saw."

His lips quirked and then smoothed out in quick succession, leaving his face too blank for my comfort. "That's an interesting assessment of the situation."

"Assessment?"

He perched on the edge of my dad's desk and scooped up a clear Lucite paperweight, transferring it from one hand to the other while he looked off to the side, likely considering his next move. Second after second passed, my ears honing in on the steady tick of the grandfather clock behind me. Pinning me with his icy blue irises, he finally asked, "Do you want to know *my* assessment of the situation?"

"Not particularly."

His lips twitched again. Damn him for finding this situation funny. "Too bad. I'm going to tell you anyway."

"Great. I can't wait," I grumbled, feeling like a child caught in a lie, and perhaps that's what I was.

"You and Salvatore D'Amico are having an affair." I opened my mouth to contradict him, and his hand sliced through the air. "Don't interrupt me. I'm not finished. As I said, you two are having an affair. While I'm not happy about it, I'm not going to punish you for it. However, I won't permit it to continue."

My teeth locked together. "How gracious of you. I'd hate for you to be forced to *punish* me."

"*Esattamente!* I'm glad we're in agreement. I want us to start our marriage with a clean slate. Until today I was a faceless man you were told you'd marry. I tried to remedy that and alleviate some of your uncertainty through our correspondence, and hopefully, I was successful. Now that we've met and we're announcing the engagement, I expect you to act like an engaged woman, which means no more alone time with Salvatore. No more longing glances, kissing, or whatever it is you do with him. All of it stops as of today. I don't want other people whispering about my fiancée's history with another man. Are we clear?"

"And are you going to act like a man engaged?" I sneered. I had eavesdropped on enough conversations to know these mafia jerks liked to have their cake and eat it too. They put their wives on a pedestal while having a woman on the side, a *goomah,* or whatever those assholes called it.

"That's only fair."

"Perfect."

"So we're on the same page?"

"Yes." I shrugged. I'd be gone in a month's time. Once we were out of here, Sal and I would have all the time in the world to be together.

"Good. Now come here and give me a kiss."

My eyes widened. "A what?"

"A kiss."

My mouth dropped open and I shuffled backward. "No."

His thick brows dropped over his glittering sapphire eyes. "I'd prefer to get the awkwardness of our first kiss out of the way in private, but have it your way. We can do it in front of a hundred or so people."

"We're not kissing in private or in front of anyone. We're announcing our engagement, eating a few appetizers, and that's it."

He tugged my hand, hauling me flush against him. I smelled his spicy citrus scent, and his body heat burned me through the layers of his fitted suit. "We're definitely kissing after the engagement toast. It's up to you whether that'll be our first kiss."

"Kissing's definitely not necessary. Everyone knows we've never met before. They don't expect us to do anything except smile, pretend to be happy, and accept this arrangement without complaint."

His arms curved around my waist, holding me firmly, his fingers tapping a mindless beat against the curve of my waist. "Oh, that's where you're wrong. It's very necessary. I need to send a clear message."

"To who? The guests? They're only here to

gossip about us later."

"I'm only interested in one guest. Salvatore needs to see firsthand that you're mine so he remembers to keep his fucking hands off my property before I cut them off."

With that warning, he bent and his lips pressed against mine, moving back and forth, demanding something I didn't want to give. Something I wasn't free to give, or at least in my mind. I tensed, making no move to retreat or reciprocate.

When he pulled back, my shoulders slumped with relief. His kiss was warm and pleasant, but it didn't set me on fire like Sal's did, and that realization vindicated my decision to run away. I was doing the right thing. Our letters were simply a bunch of sentences that didn't mean anything.

He eyed me for a few uncomfortable beats, rubbed a hand down the side of his face. "You'll do better next time."

"No, I won't. I'm not interested in kissing you to make Sal jealous. It's stupid and immature, and it won't prove a damn thing. Sal knows what's expected of me."

"I gave you a pass on whatever happened with Salvatore in the past, but if you make a fool of me today, you and Sal will not like the consequences, and I promise you, I'm a helluva lot more powerful than Salvatore. He can't protect you. In fact, neither can your father, not without pissing off all of the wrong people."

I swallowed hard, knowing he meant what he said. "No, you're right. I'll play along." *For now,* I silently added.

Marcello reached into his pocket, pulled out a dark blue velvet box, and popped it open. A ring with a square cut white diamond surround by tiny black diamonds perched between the folds of silk. My throat squeezed in on itself. I couldn't have found something I liked more if I went to the jewelry store myself, and it matched the bracelet he got me. The same one I wore every single day, keeping it tucked under the sleeves of my shirt, except today. I didn't want him to know how much I loved it.

"I'd like this to be on your finger during our announcement."

My hand came to my mouth. "I can't, Marcello. I don't feel comfortable. We barely know each other and—"

"Of course you're going to wear it. We're engaged." He slid the ring on my finger, not giving me a choice. "And I refuse to stand in front of a room full of people and announce our engagement while you have a bare finger. It'll set a precedent that I don't give a shit about my future wife and people will get it in their head that they don't have to respect you."

Resigned, I lifted one shoulder. His words made sense, or they would have if I actually intended to go marry him. "Okay, whatever you think is best."

Eyeing me with more than a little suspicion, he laced his fingers through mine. While my knee jerk reaction was to pull away, I didn't do it. Marcello could make my life a living hell if he didn't trust me or if he had any indication I planned to renege on this archaic plan he had hatched with my father.

"Are you ready to face everyone?"

"No, but I don't have a choice." I gawked at his sharp, unforgiving face. "Why are you going through with this, Marcello?"

"I have my reasons. That's all you need to know."

"Connections," I mumbled.

His eyes darkened, a muscle in his square jaw contracting, and I sensed the frustration pouring out of him. "Something like that. Now, let's go before your dad gets impatient."

CHAPTER TWENTY-EIGHT

My father flashed a brittle smile when we emerged from the study. "Is everything all set?"

"It is." Marcello placed his hand on my lower back and guided me forward.

I let him because I didn't have a choice. From the minute my eyes collided with his, I felt as if a tornado had swept into my life and flung me around without regard for the consequences.

When we entered the great room, my heart was still pounding, and my muscles were doing a good impersonation of overcooked noodles. At least a hundred sets of eyes gawked back at me, but the only one I could see was Sal.

Marcello's arm shifted, sliding around my hip, pulling me tight to his side. He grinned down at me with a look I could only describe as possessive. Then his gaze cut to Sal and the air buzzed with unexpected tension.

I didn't have time to dwell on it because my

father handed Marcello and me a glass of champagne and stepped forward, his hands raised in the air. "Family and friends, it is with great pleasure that I announce my beautiful daughter's engagement to Marcello Masciantonio. From the moment I met this man, I hoped he'd make a wonderful partner for my Emilia. From everything I've heard, he is loyal and smart. I'm overjoyed he'll be my son soon. I know my wife would've felt the same. *Salute.*"

The clinking of glasses echoed through the room, and I stood in front of everyone who was anyone in my life, completely unresponsive and lightheaded. A toxic concoction of panic, dread, and restlessness seeped into my veins, and I painted a nauseatingly fake smile on my face. As best as I could tell, no one noticed or cared. They saw what they wanted to see—a compliant daughter accepting her fate.

"To my beautiful fiancée. I can't wait to start our life together." Marcello tapped his glass against mine and I lifted it to my lips, letting the sweet bubbles pop on my tongue before sliding down my barren throat, nearly choking on it and the strange reality of life.

He set our glasses on a nearby table and cradled my face with his big calloused hands, a diabolic gleam in his eyes. Where his hard body touched mine, my skin became hot, needy. In retrospect, I should have given him what he wanted in my dad's office, and maybe he would have spared me from making a scene in front of everyone. Apprehension clawed up my chest, and I shook my head slightly, hoping I could convince him not to kiss me when I couldn't fight back without turning this whole party into a spectacle I'd never live down.

Rather than yielding to my not so subtle plea, he tightened his hold on me, and his lips slanted against mine. I stiffened, and he whispered against my mouth, "Relax and put your arms around me, little Emilia. It's only a kiss. I won't hurt you, and you won't hurt me since you promised to keep your biting tendencies in check."

My mouth parted at his joke, and he took advantage. His tongue thrust inside, kissing me, teasing me. I whimpered, and my arms tightened around his shoulders like he was the only thing keeping me standing.

My stomach danced, and my nipples hardened. Every brush of his lips or curl of his tongue turned my world upside down. All the reasons why this was a bad idea slipped my mind, and all I wanted to do was drink in everything he had to offer, damn the consequences. When we finally separated, my hands remained on his shoulders and our legs tangled like lovers. Marcello smirked, and I shut down from what could only be shock.

Light, tittering laughter pierced my kiss-induced haze, reminding me where we were. The implications of what I'd done settled deep into my bones and flames licked my face. I elbowed him, desperate to regain my sanity and keep this man at arm's length. My eyes flitted sightlessly around the room, seeking out Sal, and he was nowhere to be found.

I inhaled deeply, shoving away the guilt taunting me. Sal knew how I felt about him, and he understood what I needed to do to make the future we planned together a reality. Both of us had to play this role for another month, then we'd be free to do whatever we wanted. No price was too high for our freedom. We could do this. A few kisses wouldn't change anything.

I detached myself from my fiancé's side and wove through the crowd. I concentrated on greeting my family and my dad's business acquaintances with the expectation of losing myself in meaningless conversations and empty congratulations.

As I passed by my cousin, Gian, he grabbed my hand and pulled me into a quick embrace. "I bet your dad you wouldn't go along with this whole marriage thing, but I guess he was right and I was wrong."

I frowned. "What do you mean?"

"He thought you'd accept it without fighting too hard, and judging by that kiss, he was right. I still believe you're too young to get married though."

I rolled my eyes. "It was a kiss. It didn't mean anything. The odds are still in your favor."

His golden eyes sparkled with humor. "It didn't look that way to me."

"Yeah, well, Marcello made it clear he wasn't a man who liked to be crossed. I'm playing along for now."

"What's that supposed to mean?"

I shrugged. "Nothing you need to worry about. Go back to your date or whoever you brought with you."

"Are you kidding? I'm not dumb enough to bring

anyone within ten feet of a family event. My mom would be discussing china patterns and the benefits of a summer or winter wedding within ten minutes. And unlike you, I have no intention of settling down until I'm forty."

"Yeah, right. Your parents will ride your ass until you find some nice Italian girl who bows and scrapes anytime you enter in the room. It'll be hilarious. She'll follow you around like a puppy. *Yes, Gian. Whatever you say, Gian. Dinner's in the frig, Gian, and please wipe the lipstick off your cheek before you come to bed.*"

Even sheltered, I'd heard the rumors about Gian. He had women chasing after him wherever he went, and they all believed they'd be the one to change him. I pitied the woman who ended up married to him. Too bad I wouldn't be here to watch it all play out.

Gian burst out laughing. "*Madone*, you make me sound like an asshole."

"Aren't you?"

"You love me anyway, right little cousin?"

"That's right. You and Carmela are my favorite cousins."

"We're your only cousins."

"Exactly my point."

He hugged me again. "I know we don't spend much time together, but we're going to miss you when you move to Chicago. You'll come back to visit, right?"

A lump of emotion clogged my throat at the thought of everything I'd be giving up in a month. I'd never see my cousins, Alessandro, or my father ever again. And while my feelings for them were complex to say the least, they were all I knew. "I'll do what I can."

"Yeah." The corners of his lips jutted downward. "Lettie's looking for you."

"Gah. Can't she leave me alone?"

"Can't who leave you alone?" Marcello's hand slid around my waist, and he smiled down at me like we were a real couple and something inside of me unfurled.

"No one."

He studied me for a second. "My sister Mila wants to meet you."

"Oh, okay. I'll talk to you later, Gian."

CHAPTER TWENTY-NINE

Humming softly, I padded down the hall to my bedroom, studying the ring Marcello gave me. Tonight wasn't half bad. In another time, another place, I would probably be smitten with him, happy to get away from my father and start a new life in Chicago. His stories of his home, meeting his sister, simultaneously disarmed and charmed me. Our conversations progressed naturally and effortlessly.

When he kissed me after we toasted our engagement in front of a room full of people, I didn't feel repulsed. His lips felt...well, nice. Better than nice. At first, I panicked, questioning the strength of my feelings for Sal. As the night wore on, I chalked it up as the normal response of a woman who'd only kissed one man. It'd never happen again so I wouldn't beat myself up over it. He'd go back to Chicago in a couple of days, and shortly after that I'd fade away, never to be seen again. Tonight would be a small blip on my life's radar, soon forgotten by everyone, including me.

The thing that did concern me was that Sal left the party immediately after the toast, and I couldn't blame him. I wouldn't want to watch him parade around with another woman pretending they had a future together. Thinking about Sal with someone else made my hands ball into fists and my stomach knot. I flipped on the lamp next to my bed.

"Did you like kissing him?" Sal stepped out of the shadows, his leather loafers striking the hardwood floor with brutal thuds. Unease trickled through me.

"Holy shit. You scared me, Sal. What are you doing in here? I thought you went home."

"I drove around for an hour then I climbed into your window to wait for you."

I lifted the pearls over my head, and Sal caught my arm midway.

"Leave on the pearls and take off the ring."

I glanced at the perfectly proportioned diamond ring on my hand. I hadn't thought about it once since Marcello slipped it on my finger. It was weird how little time I'd spent with him, and yet, he managed to read me so well. I loved the jewelry he gave me. The engagement ring was delicate enough that it wouldn't interfere with playing the piano. He indulged my weird sense of humor in our letters. And his kiss...well, it'd never happen again, which meant I needed to erase it from my mind.

"You don't like it?" I lifted my hand and wiggled my fingers, trying to make light of the whole thing.

"No." His voice was strangled. Rage glimmered

in his eyes, overshadowing his usually handsome features. His cheeks were flushed and his neck corded. I inched backward, swimming in a sea of unexpected anxiety.

We stood a few feet apart. The air in my room felt chilly, and I rubbed my hands up and down my upper arms. "What's wrong? Are you mad at me?"

"Mad? I don't know. You tell me. Should I be mad at you? Would you be mad if I was hanging all over another woman in front you?"

Ducking my head, I stared at the polka dot rug beneath my feet. "Sal, you knew what was going to happen today. It's not like I kept anything from you," I whispered, feeling like I should say more or have a better excuse, only nothing came to mind. We both knew the score. We both knew the rules. I never made any promises about tonight.

He cursed under his breath, stalking toward me, pausing close enough that I could feel the heat radiating from his body. I angled my torso away from him, anticipating a verbal assault. When he didn't speak, I looked up. The anger pulsing out of him felt dirty and thick, and it stuck all over me like a wet blanket.

Sal murmured, "I couldn't stand seeing his hands and lips on you, Em. I wanted to kill him. Tear him apart with my bare hands. Can you imagine the crazy shit going through my head?" He captured a strand of my hair, curling it around his finger.

I swallowed hard, barely able to complete the action. "I did what I had to."

"Are you having second thoughts? Did you change your mind about marrying him? If that's what you want, I won't fight you." He tipped his head to the ceiling, his face bleak, his shoulders bunched tight. "Fuck, even saying that makes me sick to my stomach."

"No, Sal." I tugged on the lapels of his jacket so tight like I could force him to retract his gallant offer. I didn't want gallant. I wanted someone who'd fight for me at any cost. "How could you think that? Do you have any idea how much I lo—" I paused mid-word. "How much you mean to me?"

"I tried so hard, Em. I honestly did. But I don't want to wait any longer."

"Wait for what?" I choked out.

"I need you. All of you. I need to know you're mine. I want you so damn much. I'd do anything for you. If you only knew how you've changed me…" He pulled me closer to him.

I sucked in a breath as his lips came within millimeters of mine. My promise to Marcello rattled around in my brain like an omen. A chill whizzed down my spinal column, and I shoved aside the trickle of guilt and focused on Sal. On us. On this flicker in time.

With a sliver of the fading daylight peeking through my blinds, his hands circled me, slowly releasing the zipper at the back of my dress. The soft buzz sounded more pronounced in my ears, almost as if my father and anyone else lingering on the floor below us could hear it. Or sense it.

He pushed the dress from my arms, and it pooled on the black and white rug, a lacy lavender wreath around my ankles. Feeling exposed and vulnerable, my arms went to my small breasts, hiding them from his greedy gaze.

"You're so damn beautiful, Em. I can't believe you're real."

He removed the gun holster from his waist and shrugged out of his suit jacket and snowy white dress shirt. A dark thatch of hair stretched from the bottom of his navel, arrowing into the waistband of his pants. My fingers tingled with the need to touch him, and for the first time, I knew he wouldn't deny me.

He lifted me, his hands gripping my hips, and I circled my legs around his waist. The warm skin of his hard chest met my breasts, soft against hard, and we both sucked in a breath. He marched me backward and laid me on the bed.

His tongue slid against the seam of my mouth. I opened eagerly, and he deepened the kiss. His hips rocking slowly between my thighs, I held tight to his waist. Ready to explode with need, Sal's mouth skated down my neck, paying homage to the sensitive skin beneath my ear and at the hollow of my throat. My entire body vibrated with a mishmash of need and fear of the unknown.

The pads of his fingers swept down my ribcage, rounding my hips as he pulled my nipple into his mouth. His teeth and tongue tag teamed the sensitive point and my head rolled to the side, an exaggerated moan falling from my lips. Something about the softness of his mouth contrasting with the roughness of his teeth and stubble set me on fire.

"Oh, God, Sal."

"I know. I know," he mumbled and I could feel his lips curve into a smile against my skin.

My jittery hands fumbled with his belt buckle. The sound of clanking metal and the swoosh of leather echoed in the silence of my bedroom. I tugged on Sal's zipper, fusing his mouth to mine. I released him from his pants, running my closed palm up and down his smooth velvet flesh, thick and hard. The instant his hand slipped inside my panties, I arched my hips greedy for more.

"Mmm," I mumbled.

My eyes drifted closed, and I gave in to Sal. My engagement, kissing another man—all of it faded away like a hazy dream. We morphed into a flurry of tangled body parts, greedy hands, and seeking lips. Whimpers of need intertwined with stuttered breaths.

He nipped my ear. "Did it feel this good when he kissed you?"

All the heat building inside of me turned to ice, and I buried my hands in the silky-smooth duvet beneath me. Images of Marcello downstairs having a drink with my father freeze-framed through my brain, and the unease of my betrayal and dishonesty slithered through me. I had no intention of marrying Marcello, but being with Sal like this smacked of cheating, and something about that made me extremely uncomfortable. I wiggled my hips and pushed at his chest, trying to get out from underneath him.

"Sal," I rasped, "we need to stop. We can't do this."

He raised his weight onto his forearms. "What's wrong? Did I hurt you?"

"No, it not that. It's just that…you were right all

along. Having sex with you right now would be a mistake."

His eyes of a thousand different colors narrowed until all I could see were his black pupils. "What do you mean? You're the one who told me we should do what we want. What's changed?"

I dragged my hand up my forehead and smoothed back my hair. "I know. I know, but I wasn't thinking clearly. We need to wait until we don't have all of this drama hanging over our heads."

"This is about him. He charmed you into thinking he's a good guy. That he's not half bad." He climbed to his feet, stuffing himself back into his pants. "God, Em. He's a prick. I wasn't going to tell you this, but he brought his fucking mistress to your engagement party. Everyone knew it too. Think about that. You're choosing him over me, and he doesn't even respect you enough to break things off with her or come alone. If he can't stomach being away from her for a few days, you can be damn sure he'll shove her in your face every chance he gets after you're married."

"His mistress?"

My stomach tilted. What kind of sick game was Marcello playing? He gave me this whole speech about breaking things off with Sal, accepting the past and moving on with no hard feelings while his girlfriend was waiting outside the door.

"Yeah, the brunette in the emerald green dress. He's been seeing her for years, but he can't marry her. She's not Italian. She's some stripper from one of his clubs in Chicago, so if you're doing this for him, your loyalty is wildly misplaced. He doesn't care about you. You're a box to be checked on his way to becoming the head of the outfit."

I yanked the throw blanket to my chin covering my trembling body, needing armor to conceal all the sickening emotions rioting inside of me. While I hadn't changed my mind about marrying Marcello, my feelings toward him had softened. God, I was a horrible judge of character. Every word out of his mouth was a lie, and I didn't have a clue. How pathetic. Part of me wanted to have sex with Sal solely to one up Marcello. I couldn't be with him out of spite, though. I'd only be cheating Sal and me.

"I'm never going to marry him, so it doesn't matter if he paraded every woman he's ever touched in front of me. I don't care."

"Then, why are you pushing me away?" He paced beside the bed. "I care about you so damn much, Emilia. I've waited for you. I haven't pushed you for more until now. What else do you want me to do?"

"Nothing. I trust you completely. But being with you tonight like this doesn't feel right, especially when I stood in front of all of my friends and family a couple of hours ago and misled them into believing I would marry Marcello." I swallowed hard, tears stinging the backs of my eyes. "It feels dirty. I don't want to taint our relationship with him. When we're finally together, I want it to be about us and what we feel for each other. I'm not telling you it won't happen until we're out of this place, but I don't want it to be a reaction to your jealousies or my insecurities."

Sal linked his hands behind his neck and lifted his face to the ceiling. "No, you're right. Sorry I pushed this. The last thing I want is to hurt you or make you uncomfortable."

Still clinging to the blanket, I scooted to the edge of the bed, threw my legs over the side, and wrapped one arm around him. "Thanks for understanding. I know I'm probably giving you whiplash with all my back and forth."

"Shh." His knuckles trailed down my neck. "It's okay. I don't care if it happens tonight or six months from now. I love you and—"

My heart sped up erratically, and I met his heavy stare. "You love me?"

He chuckled. "Of course I do. What do you think all this is about? I wouldn't risk my life and my family's life if I didn't love you."

"Will something happen to your family if we go through with this?"

"They'll be okay. My brother's going to college next year, and my mom has a job now. I'm not worried about them."

I frowned. "You promise?"

He cupped the side of my face and kissed the tip of my nose. "I'll miss them, sure, but I'd miss you more if I didn't go with you. You're my future."

"You're mine too," I replied, ruthlessly suppressing the memory of the man who uttered those exact words so many years ago. Sal loved me. I loved him, and that was all I needed to make a new life. A perfect life with the one person who loved me enough to give up everything. My mom would have approved.

CHAPTER THIRTY

Marcello extended his visit so he could celebrate my birthday with me in less than a week. My father vetoed all of my carefully crafted objections to this change of plans. Apparently, Marcello wanted to get to know me better. I didn't give a shit either way except that it gave me less time to prepare my getaway and finalize plans with Sal.

"Dinner was great," Marcello said to my father. "Thanks for inviting me, Dominick."

"No problem. Emilia and I like having company for dinner. It's only been the two of us for so long."

I checked the urge to roll my eyes, knowing the childish gesture wouldn't win any points with my father. If he wanted to sit here acting like a happy family that was his prerogative. In reality, he barely bothered to join me for dinner on most nights, and when he did, it usually involved takeout or a meal prepared by Bianca, our sometimes housekeeper slash cook. The only thing the past dinners with my father and tonight had in common was strained silence.

Tonight, Bianca made a seafood *brodetto* with grilled bread. Neither my dad nor I were big fans of seafood, but evidently Marcello requested it. So here we sat, picking at our bowl of five or six kinds of fish drenched in basil heavy tomato sauce. Luckily, Bianca had added plenty of red pepper and garlic to mask the fishy smell, and I succeeded in gagging down enough bites to stave off my hunger until I got to my room where I could munch on the snacks hidden in my desk drawer.

Marcello pointed his spoon at me. "You don't like it?"

"It's okay. I'm not that hungry." *For this or the company,* I wordlessly added.

For three nights, Marcello had rattled off question after question like a job interview, and I did my best to answer without revealing my distaste for this whole charade, the best description for what was happening. I acted as if I had every intention of going through with this arranged marriage, and he pretended he didn't have his mistress tucked away in his hotel room or wherever he was staying.

"Emilia eats like a bird," my dad interjected.

God, I hated when he brought up my eating habits or my size. It made me sound like some neurotic head case. I ate plenty, and as for being small, so was my mom. Except for my coloring and hair, I didn't get much of anything from him. On occasion, I wished I had inherited some of his height, but more often, I was thankful I didn't resemble him physically. Since my mom died, I hated him more than I liked him, so it'd suck if I saw him every time I glanced in a mirror.

I placed my spoon beside my plate. "May I be excused?"

My father tossed his napkin on the table. "Not tonight, sweetheart. I have some business to take care of so I asked Marcello to stick around until I get back."

"That's not necessary. Sal can—"

"Sal's busy. He can't sit around babysitting you anymore."

I glared at Marcello from under my lashes; his stoic face revealed nothing. What did he say to my father about Sal?

"Marcello, I'm sure you have stuff you want to do," I said. "I'll be fine here by myself, and I won't be very good company. I'm probably going to watch T.V. for an hour, then go to bed."

He lifted and dropped one shoulder like he didn't care. "I don't have anything more important to do than spend time with you. That's why I'm here. When we're back in Chicago, I'll be working late most nights, so we might as well make good use of our time together now."

I gritted my teeth, biting back a boatload of rejoinders that would only make this visit more awkward. "You want to watch a movie?"

"I had something else in mind."

"You did?"

He stood and held his hand out to me. "I was hoping I could hear you play the piano again."

Eyeing his outreached palm like a snake ready to bite, I swallowed back my nervous energy. I hadn't stepped foot in the music room since my father had unilaterally canceled my lessons. I attributed my lack of interest to being busy with my escape plan. In truth, I had a hard time accepting how drastically my life had changed in the past year. My father crushed my dream of reaching my mom's level of success as a concert pianist without a second thought.

When my mom died, I poured all my energy into becoming the type of musician who would make her proud. For years I questioned whether I truly loved to play the piano. Sadly, it took my father taking away the option to realize how much I wanted it.

Even if I succeeded in getting away from here, I'd never be able to play anywhere that would bring attention to me. For the rest of my life, I had to accept I'd only be able to play in private settings with close friends. I'd never walk in my mom's footsteps or become her legacy.

Reluctantly, I took his hand and stood. A little zing of electricity shot up my arm and I blinked, heaving in a deep breath and forcing my wayward reaction to him into submission. "I'm rusty. I haven't played in months. Is there anything I can do to convince you to take a raincheck?"

"Don't be rude to your fiancé, Emilia." My father pushed back his chair, the wooden legs scraping loudly over the hardwood floor. "You started playing before your feet could reach the pedals, and if he wants to hear you, then you might as well put all the money spent on your ridiculous hobby to use. I'll see you in the morning."

Without so much as a wave or a backward glance, he headed toward the garage. Stunned, I stood unmoving, listening to the slam of the door, the telltale hum of the garage door opener, and the rumble of his car engine. I couldn't believe he called playing the piano a silly hobby. Every word of encouragement he'd uttered about my one and only talent was a lie. He never gave a shit. I shouldn't be surprised, but it still hurt.

"I'd love for you to play "Moonlight" by Beethoven again, even a little of it," Marcello said, interrupting my self-pitying inner monologue.

I smiled, grateful he didn't bring up my father's comment. "You remember what I played that night?"

"Among other things."

He flashed a tiny but coaxing smile and my belly thawed like I'd swallowed a mouthful of rich, warm coffee. I didn't understand how this man could simultaneously unnerve and comfort me.

"All right, but you have to promise not to laugh if I make a fool of myself. I hate someone to listening to me when I'm not at my best."

"You'll do fine. Either way, it'd be a pleasure to hear you play again."

CHAPTER THIRTY-ONE

Marcello followed me into the spare bedroom my father had converted into a music room after my mom died. I perched on the gleaming cherry wood bench and opened the lid. My eyes closed, I trailed my fingers over the ivory keys, drew in a breath, and played for the first time in months.

At first my fingers stumbled, fat-fingering the keys, and I sighed in frustration, shocked how quickly my playing had gone downhill. When I moved to close the lid, Marcello put his hands on top of mine.

"Relax, little Emilia. It's only me here. No judgment, no expectations. Just two people spending time together."

I swallowed back my reservations and replaced my fingers. "Okay, but don't blame me if your ears are bleeding by the end."

"I'll live."

After his gentle words, everything fell into place

like it had been days since I last touched a piano. Time flew by, my body swaying to the melody. After I completed the piece, I was surprised I had made it through without any major missteps. I glanced at Marcello to gauge his reaction. The way he looked at me with his heavy-lidded speculative eyes buried in the rugged angles of his face made my stomach knot.

"Beautiful," he said in his smoky voice as he stepped out of the shadows.

Mesmerized by the odd light in Marcello's eyes, I made no effort to break the silence in the room. A chill inched up my back at the thought of all of the dark secrets hidden beneath his veil of civility. Something must have made him that way. My gut told me he was a man who'd done all kinds of things that would rock me to the core. Even knowing that, I couldn't deny that Marcello intrigued me. He was a firestorm of beauty, violence, and power.

I released a careful breath, tamping down the weird feelings blooming inside of me. "Thank you."

"Why'd you stop playing?"

I glanced to the side, and after a beat, I answered, "It's complicated."

He dropped his hands on the top of my shoulders and I swallowed audibly. His heady masculine scent surrounded me, producing a mild case of vertigo. "We have time for complicated. Your dad won't be back for hours."

"Weird things happened." I stared bitterly at the piano. "Confrontations with strangers. I don't know. Dumb stuff I didn't understand. My father didn't think it was safe for me to spend much time away from the house, and now I'm basically a prisoner in my home."

"Ah." He worked his fingers into my shoulders, massaging my tight muscles. While I should keep my distance from him both mentally and physically, his touch felt too good and I surrendered to it, dropping my chin to my chest. His fingers dipped into the scooped neck of my blouse, leisurely mapping the horizontal lines of my collarbone. "You'll have more freedom when you move to Chicago. I want you to get to know my friends and family and make a life there. You can take as many lessons as you want and perform whenever and wherever."

Acting purely on instinct, I leaned into him, my body brushing against his silky tie. His warm, minty breath stirred the fallen strands of hair next to my ear. One of his hands slipped up my back, tracing my spine and the curve of my waist. My eyes fluttered shut, getting lost in the moment. Goose bumps peppered my arms. A crackling energy swirled around the room.

When his fingertips brushed the underside of my breast, an alarm sounded inside my brain, muted by the slow burn of desire. If I encouraged him, he'd kiss me or more. I straightened my back and pitched my torso away from him, desperate to slow the wave of need sucking me under.

"So you don't care what I do. Once we're married you'll have your alliance with my family, and both of us can go our own way. Live our own lives," I said, turning his generous words on their head and using them as ammunition.

His hands tensed, his fingers digging into my flesh, then he backed away, severing all contact, his posture deceptively casual and relaxed. "Where'd you get that idea?"

I lurched to my feet and whirled around. "I know that you brought your girlfriend, *goomah* or whatever, to our engagement party, which tells me you have no intention of having a real marriage with me, which is fine. I don't want to marry you either. I'm too young, and I don't know you, but I'd appreciate it if you stopped toying with my emotions."

He frowned. "Emilia..."

"No. I'm not done talking. I don't care if we have a real marriage. I don't even care if you plan to set me up in another house. But I do object to you pretending you're interested in more than my last name and connections. It's a waste of our time and energy. So here's what I think. You can go home, do what you want, and I'll do what I want here."

His lips twitched, and he wiped his hand over his mouth.

I shot him a scathing look. "What's so funny?"

"My girlfriend. You think I brought my girlfriend?"

I jutted out my hip and lifted my chin. "I know you brought your girlfriend. She was the woman in the green dress. Right?"

"Sarah?"

"I don't know her name. No one introduced her to me."

"Did you want me to introduce her to you?"

"Ah, let me think." I tapped my finger on my lips. "Um, yeah, I'll pass, but thanks for the offer." *Asshole*. Thank God, I had no intention of marrying this man. I'd be silently plotting his death within a year.

"Contrary to what you apparently think of me," he drawled, his voice deep and mocking, "I'm not so insecure that I need a woman hanging off my arm and in my bed to feel better about myself. And I hate to point this out, but your accusation is a little hypocritical given Sal's presence."

"So you're saying you've never touched that woman?" I folded my arms across my chest and tipped up my chin, determinedly ignoring my hypocrisy because he nailed it on the head. I had no right to toss accusations at him for more reasons than he knew. "Is that what you want me to believe?"

Lazy amusement lit his face. "Are you jealous, little Emilia?"

"What? You can't be serious. I don't care what or who you do. I only want to know what to expect so I'm not blindsided by your girlfriends at every turn."

Stalking closer to me, his eyes darkened with an edgy power, and I backpedaled until the piano dug into my back. His hands flattened on top of the piano on either side of me, effectively caging me in. "Is that a fact?" A hard, possessive tone colored his voice, making me hyper aware of our proximity.

"Yes," I managed to squeak out, my voice barely a thread of a sound. He cupped the back of my neck, bringing his mouth within striking distance, and my heart misfired. "But you know what? This is irrelevant. I don't have a clue why I brought her up. Let's talk about something else."

"She's not my girlfriend. She came with one of my associates."

"And you never—" I couldn't finish my question, mostly because I didn't want to know the answer. I shouldn't care either way, and the fact that I did even a little bit scared the crap out of me. Marcello wasn't my future. He'd never be anything to me other than a short-lived flash in time before I started living the life I always wanted.

I closed my eyes, gambling that if I didn't see his ruggedly handsome face, I could erase all of the disconcerting emotions spinning inside of me. Unfortunately, he took it as an invitation. He pressed his lips against mine with a single-minded hunger, his arms hooked around my waist, and I felt the hard imprint of his body flush against mine.

His tongue swept into my mouth, warm and malleable, and the heat around us multiplied tenfold. His erection pressed into my belly and desire stretched my nerve endings like a rubber band begging to snap. His hands traveled recklessly up and down my sides, and an achy need washed over me. I drew my legs together, pouring every ounce of confusion, longing, and frustration into the kiss. I slipped my hands around his waist and under his jacket, caressing his ropy muscles and clung to him as if he were the only thing keeping me from crashing to the floor.

While I knew deep in my gut this was wrong on too many levels to name, I rationalized it as a goodbye and an apology for my deception all rolled into one. I got lost in his taste, his smell, and him. A soft moan reverberated through the room and not until I felt his lips pull into a smile did I realize it came from me.

Too long yet too soon, he pulled away, his chest heaving, his blue eyes hooded, and his lips swollen. He looked insanely beautiful, like a bronzed Roman god. I rested my face against his chest, listening to the steady thud of his heart. The kiss combined with the feel of his arms around me and the soft purr of our breaths lulled me into some strange bubble where nothing existed except the dark, sensual pull between the two of us. His hand roamed all over me, dominance, power and sex rolling off him like a voodoo love spell, weakening my objections to him. To the idea of us, and the future he talked about years earlier in the dimly lit hall outside my father's study.

"As tempting as you are, little Emilia, I should go before we take this too far. I don't think Dominick would appreciate me taking advantage of our time alone."

His comment snapped me back into reality. The fact that he believed this might lead to more between us hit me like a kick to the gut. My body's reaction to this man eviscerated me. It was completely out of sync with the future I planned for myself, and yet none of that made a difference within seconds of him touching me.

"Oh, yeah, whatever you think," I said, embarrassment creeping up my face. I looked away from his too keen eyes and focused on the black and white photo of my family hanging on the wall. My father had stripped the house of every last reminder of our family after my mom died except for that picture.

Marcello reached for me, framing my face, simultaneously forcing me to look at him and acknowledge this thing between us—whatever it was or wasn't.

"Before too long, we'll have plenty of time to get to know each other and much more freedom to do it."

I shrugged out of his hold and squared my shoulders, mentally trampling on the hysteria inching through me. "I assume you can let yourself out. I'm not feeling very social anymore."

He cocked his head to the side. "So it's going to be like that, huh?"

"I have no idea what you're talking about."

"Every time we make progress and I think we're on the same page, you retreat into your shell again."

"No amount of you forcing yourself on me will change the fact that I don't want to marry you, and I'd appreciate if you kept your hands and lips off me."

"You can ignore what's happening between us all you want, but it won't change reality."

"Leave."

"Not until you admit you liked kissing me."

"No." I'd never admit anything because I hated that my body betrayed me every time he touched me. The way my silly heart hammered and my limbs trembled made me sick.

The muscles in the lower half of his jaw ticked,

and we both stood rooted to the floor, our invisible swords drawn, preparing to do battle. The air around us shifted, thickening and pressing against my ribcage, making it impossible to fill my lungs.

I opened my mouth, and his knuckles brushed the side of my temple, lowering my guard and scattering the words on the tip of my tongue. "If you deny it, I'm not opposed to practicing with you until you change your mind."

"Why are you doing this?" I croaked, not caring if I sounded weak. I wanted him to leave me alone and stop messing with me. I had already planned out my life, and it didn't include him. Could never include him.

"Why are you resisting?"

"So many reasons, but mostly because I have no interest in doing my father's bidding."

He chuckled. "And that's what you think you're doing by agreeing to marry me?"

"Aren't I?"

He pulled me into his arms and kissed me, quick and dirty. "You have a lot to learn, little Emilia. I'll see you tomorrow."

I gaped at him as he exited the room, the herringbone hardwood floor creaking under the weight of his leather-soled shoes. I stared until his broad shoulders disappeared around the corner. When I heard the alarm chime and the front door shut, I finally found the courage to make my way to my bedroom.

CHAPTER THIRTY-TWO

My legs wobbly and my heart chugging a guilty beat, I shut my bedroom door behind me. I flattened my back against the white painted wooden panels on my wall.

"What a mess," I mumbled.

I needed to yank my head out of the clouds and pull myself together. Without fail, Marcello turned my world upside down and set it on fire every single time I was alone with him. Somehow he wove a spell around me, making me forget why I wanted to reinvent myself far away from here. Worst of all, though, I forgot about Sal, and I freakin' loved Sal. How could I not? He planned to give up his whole life, his family, his future for me. That counted for something. A whole helluva lot of something, especially when Marcello wasn't giving up anything.

I tugged on the roots of my hair, taking comfort in the stinging sensation. It helped me focus and remember what mattered, and that was Sal and the promises we made to each other. I needed to talk to him and hear his voice, but I wouldn't put it past my father to monitor my phone, and making him suspicious was the last thing I needed.

"*Mannaggia.*"

I threw myself face down onto my bed, and then I remembered Sal gave me three burner phones. Practically stumbling in my haste to get to the duffel bag hidden in my walk-in closet, I flew across the room. In less than thirty seconds, I had one of the black phones in hand and I was dialing Sal's number.

I settled onto the floor and kicked the closet door closed, waiting for him to answer. Listening to ring after ring, my attention bounced around the small space. The yellowish overhead light made my clothes, all various shades of gray and black, resemble a sepia photograph.

When I had resigned myself to leaving a message, Sal answered.

"*Hello.*"

Music and laughter floated through my phone. I pulled my knees tighter to my chest, digging the fingers of my free hand into the fleshy part next to my shinbone.

"Sal, it's me," I whispered in case my father suddenly came home and decided to venture in the direction of my room.

"*I'll call you back,*" he barked into the phone, his voice curt.

What the hell?

Like they had a mind of their own, tears beaded

at the corners of my eyes, determined to make a fool of me. Frustrated, I tossed shoe after shoe at the light switch until I hit the lower half, successfully shrouding the closet in darkness. For reasons I couldn't explain, my emotional rollercoaster felt less loony when I couldn't see a damn thing.

Over a half an hour later, the phone rang.

"Emilia," Sal said, his voice rushed and urgent, *"are you okay? Did something happen?"*

"No. I'm fine." I molded into the wall of hanging clothes behind me. "I needed to hear your voice. I miss you."

"I miss you too."

Neither of us said another word. His soft breaths poured through the speaker along with a roar of an engine and the honking of a horn.

"Where are you?"

"I'm leaving your dad's club."

"Oh." I licked my lips. "You were working tonight?"

"I'm always working. I have a lot of work to catch up on now that I'm not following you around every day. How are things with your fiancé?" His question came out like a sneer, and it took a few seconds for me to respond.

"Um, well, they're okay. He left a little bit ago. He wants to spend as much time as possible together before he leaves, so I'm stuck for now."

"That sounds fun."

I pinched the bridge of my nose, sadness rippling through me. While I didn't want things to be like this between us, I couldn't figure out how to make it better. Circumstances beyond our control had stacked the odds against us, and I was starting to suspect nothing would change it. Maybe some things weren't meant to be. As quickly as the realization floated through my mind, I swatted it away. Nothing was worse than defeatist thinking.

"Not really."

"Did you kiss him again?"

"Sal." I drew out his name and punctuated it with a sigh. He was already mad at me about the stupid kiss at our engagement party. There was no reason to add fuel to his jealousy. "We already talked about this. I'm doing what I have to do so we can be together, and I've never initiated a single kiss."

"So that's a yes." A chuckle laced with enough bitterness to tilt my stomach trickled into my ear. *"Did you ask him about his girlfriend? Or don't you care that he's making a fool out of you?"*

"I asked him about Sarah, and he's not making a fool out of me because we'll be gone soon. He's the one who will look ridiculous."

"What'd he say?"

I rolled forward and stretched on my belly, my bare feet tucked in between the wall of dresses hanging from the rod. I rested my forehead on my forearm. "That they were friends and she was there with one of his associates. That's it."

"You actually believe him?"

Strangely, I did trust Marcello's explanation. He didn't offer me anything other than his word and a flimsy explanation, and yet, something compelled me to have faith in him.

"I didn't give him the third degree or anything. So yeah, whatever."

He snorted. *"Okaaay. So he tells you a lie, and you accept it. Jesus, Em, he's walking all over you, and you don't give a shit. She probably waits for him in his hotel room every night and they laugh at how naïve you are."*

"And tell me why I should care again? In another couple of weeks I'll never see him again so he can do whatever he wants with whomever he wants. I don't love him. I don't even *know* him. Why do you keep bringing it up? Are you having second thoughts or something?"

My stomach knotted, recognizing the deceit in my words. Even though I didn't like it, Marcello evoked feelings in me that were becoming harder to deny. Feelings that urged me to turn my back on my plans and take a chance on him. Feelings that threw an uncomfortable spotlight on the chinks in my relationship with Sal. Feelings I desperately hoped would vanish entirely once Sal and I left together.

"Shit, Em. No. You're right. I'm sorry I keep bringing it up. I can't stand this."

"Me neither, but it's almost over, and he's leaving soon."

"When?"

"After my birthday."

"Three more days. God, that seems like a lifetime."

"Yeah. Why don't you come over tomorrow? My dad's not going to kick you out if you show up on his doorstep."

"We both know that's not a good idea."

"Why? What's the worst that could happen?"

"Are you serious? Marcello could come after me

again. He's a fuckin' lunatic."

"Wait." I scrambled to my feet. "What do you mean come after you again? Did something happen that you're not telling me about?"

"He stopped by the bar after he left your house and we exchanged some words tonight. Things got a little heated and he took a cheap shot at me. I'm fine. No need to make a big deal about it."

I squeezed the phone until the edges of my hard shell case dug into my palm. "Jesus, Sal. I'm sorry. When he asked about us, I had no idea he'd confront you."

I heard his tires squeal, followed by a loud thump that sounded like his hand slammed against the steering wheel. *"The fuck? You seriously told him about us?"*

"He knew. He saw us at my piano concert." The silence thickened, and I wondered if he disconnected the call. "Sal, are you there?"

"I'm here." His voice sounded strained.

"Are you mad?"

"Mad? I don't even...what the hell were you thinking?"

"He said he didn't care the about my past as long as it didn't happen again."

He scoffed. *"And you believed him?"*

The silence stretched thick and heavy, adding more than physical distance between us. More than ever, my plan to run off into the sunset with Sal felt like a house of cards. One unpredictable wind and everything would collapse.

"Yeah, I did. I guess I wasn't thinking."

Sal sighed. *"No, don't worry about it. It's not*

your fault. I'll see what I can do about stopping by tomorrow. I have a birthday present for you and since your party was canceled, I need to find a way to give it to you."

"You didn't have to get me anything. Running away with me is the only present I need."

"Too late. It's already wrapped."

"Okay, then. See you tomorrow." Only after I hung up did I remember he said my father had canceled my birthday party.

CHAPTER THIRTY-THREE

"Aren't you hungry?" Marcello asked.

I looked up from my lasagna. The cheese had morphed into a congealed mess over the last thirty minutes. With my stomach twisted into knots, I couldn't eat more than a few bites. Sal had ignored all of my texts and calls for the last two days, and he hadn't stopped by to see me. My relationship with Sal was crumbling, and I had no one to blame except myself.

Over the last week, Marcello had systematically kissed me into idiocy, and I lost touch with why I wanted to skip out on this life minute-by-minute. Everything about him—his touch, his smiles, his voice—felt right and wrong at the same time.

"Huh?"

He gestured to my plate. "You haven't taken more than a bite. Your father said this was your favorite. I could've ordered something else."

"It is her favorite," my dad interjected. I hated

how he hovered over us, watching and commenting on every interaction like he had nothing better to do.

I laid my fork diagonally across my plate, the ringing sound unnaturally loud in the cavernous dining room. "Sorry. It's just…well, I was thinking about my birthday tomorrow."

My father leaned back, folding his arms across his chest and his red and black checked tie bent sideways. "What about it?"

"I talked to Sal a couple of days ago." From the corner of my eye, I caught the frosty look Marcello directed at my dad. "He thought you canceled my party. Did you disinvite him?"

"No."

"Then why did he say you had?"

"Because I canceled the party entirely."

My puzzled gaze met my father's. "Why?"

He took a deep sip of his ruby red wine and shifted in his seat. "I wanted to get through dinner and dessert before we discussed this."

"Discussed what?"

Marcello dropped his napkin on the table and pushed back his chair, the legs scraping against the floor and putting me on edge. "Emilia," he finally said, "I have decided it would be best if you left with me tomorrow night."

Dread inched up my throat. "Tomorrow? I can't leave with you tomorrow," I said, shaking my head adamantly. "I have things to do. I'm not ready. I'm not even packed. How can you expect me to leave my home of nearly nineteen years with less than twenty-four hours' notice?"

"It's settled. I already bought you a plane ticket.

You will be staying with my sister until we get married."

"No." I jumped out of my chair, and it tumbled backward. "Did you hear anything I said? I haven't packed. I haven't said goodbye to my friends and family and—"

Marcello arched an eyebrow. "Sal?"

Swallowing hard, I glanced at the floor. "Sal doesn't have anything to do with this. This is about us."

A harsh sound tore from his lips, and he clenched his teeth together, his expression stony. "This is the way it has to be. It's best if you make a clean break from your life here. You can come back and visit in a year or two when you have settled into your new life."

Pain ricocheted through my chest like a pinball. Bending forward, I clutched the edge of the dining room table. "I don't want to leave. Does that count for nothing? Does what I want matter at all? Why are you two so intent or ruining my life?"

"Emilia, don't embarrass yourself or me." My father got up and circled the table, pausing in front of me. "You're out of options, and this is what's best for our family. I wish things were different, but there's nothing I can do about it."

"This isn't the eighteenth century. You don't get to force me to marry someone. I am my own person, not a piece on a chessboard to move as you see fit."

My father sighed, his chest heaving outward. He looked weary with the dark circles under his eyes and his pinched mouth. "Marcello's promised to take care of you, and he'll be able to give you more freedom than you have here. He's arranged for you to resume your piano lessons under a famous pianist, Martha Giles. You've probably heard of her. She's fantastic, almost as good as your mother. You can start performing again. You'll have a nice life there. You'll see." He forced a smile.

The corners of my eyes burned. "Why are you doing this to me, Dad? What did I do to make you hate me so much?"

"Don't look at this as a punishment. Look at it as an opportunity. You can start over in Chicago without the shadow of your mother's death or the Trassato name hanging over your head. Marcello will take care of you."

My heart breaking, I pressed my hand to the front of my shirt, imagining I could hold the shattered pieces together. "But I don't love him. I love Sal. I know you don't want to hear—"

The open palm of my father's hand collided with my cheek. "Don't act like a spoiled child, Emilia. I raised you better, and this is bigger than you and what you want. You need to show some respect."

Pain radiated through me, and I reeled backward, cupping my face with my hand and pointing a finger at my father with the other. "I hate you. I can see why Mom killed herself to get away from you. I'd do the same thing if you were my husband. Oh, wait, maybe I got that wrong. Maybe you stuffed those pills down her throat so she couldn't leave you. I heard what she said that night. She wanted out of this life, and you didn't give a shit about her *or* our family. You only cared about power and money, and that hasn't changed. She hated you, and

I can certainly understand why. You're a monster incapable of love. You might as well be a fucking robot. As for respect, respect is won not demanded, and you haven't won mine."

His mouth twisted into a snarl. "Shut your mouth. You don't know a damn thing about my relationship with your mother. And as for this marriage, I did everything I could to find another way."

"Dominick," Marcello snapped, his hand coming down on my father's shoulder, hard and unforgiving, "I need to talk to you."

They headed toward the entryway, stopping in my line of sight, but far enough that I wouldn't be able to hear their conversation word for word. Marcello rested his hip against the wall, his blue eyes glittering with so much hatred my breath caught.

A scorching tirade in Italian spewed from Marcello's mouth, and I silently cursed myself for refusing to continue my language lessons after the third grade. While I knew some slang, phrases, and enough to have a shallow conversation, Marcello's rapid-fire words made no sense. My father's answer was short and curt. Marcello gestured to the front door and switched to English to tell him to give us some time alone. My father's lips thinned and he walked right past me without making eye contact.

"Where are you going?" I called after him.

"Out. I'll be home late. Don't wait up for me." His far-reaching strides ate up the floor, and the service door to the garage slammed shut less than a minute later.

CHAPTER THIRTY-FOUR

Marcello crossed the room and righted my chair at the kitchen table. "Sit."

I was more than a little bewildered by what I witnessed. Nobody treated my dad like that, and if they tried, he made damn sure they were six feet under so it wouldn't happen again. Yet, after a few harsh sentences, he caved to Marcello. I didn't get it.

He tapped his fingers on the wooden-slatted back. "Please."

"What happened with my dad?" I slipped into the chair rather than argue with him. If the last minutes told me anything, it was that my rebellion would be futile. Complying was the fastest way to end this interaction.

"Not yet."

He moved into the kitchen, opening cabinet after cabinet.

"Can I help you find something?"

He popped up holding a clear bottle and two shot glasses. "I found it."

"What's that?"

"Sambuca. My *nonna* made me drink it when I didn't feel well."

"She gave you shots of alcohol?" I said, utterly incredulous.

"Not shots, more like a tablespoon here or there. Don't knock it until you try it."

He set everything on the table next to me and filled the glasses until they were seeping over the rim.

I waved my hand flippantly. "I'm not going to drink that crap. It tastes like black licorice."

He slid one of the glasses closer to me with two long fingers, leaving a small puddle of clear liquid pooling on top of the table. "So what's your point?"

"I hate black licorice."

"Humor me."

I rolled my eyes. Somehow this man always found a way to trick me into forgetting my bad mood.

"One shot and then you'll leave, and I'll go to bed."

"Three."

"No."

"Yes. Three shots for three truths. You can ask me three questions about anything. For every answer I give you, you'll take a shot and vice versa."

"Two truths," I countered.

"Two truths and three shots. One before we start, the rest with each question."

My eyes narrowed. "Are you trying to get me drunk?"

"Three shots won't do anything except help you relax."

I raised my hands in the air. "In case you haven't noticed, I don't weigh that much."

"You'll be fine." He nudged my glass with his knuckle and lifted his glass to his lips. "Ready?"

I poured the syrupy liquid between my lips, holding it in my mouth for a few seconds, and then let it slide down my throat. He followed suit. When the last drop hit my tongue, I placed the shot glass on the table accompanied by a *thud*. I shimmied my shoulders to ward off the warm, fuzzy sensation. He refilled both of our glasses.

"You first," I prompted him.

"What do you know about the motivations for our marriage?"

I dropped my gaze to the floor. "Nothing, except that it must somehow benefit your family and mine."

"You didn't hear any details when I found you hiding outside of your dad's office that night?"

"No, nothing but raised voices. Is there something I should know?"

He chugged another shot of Sambuca, his peacock blue gaze skittering to my mouth, then back to my eyes. "Is that your question? Because it's a little subjective."

"Fine. Then, I'll ask the same question I've been asking since our engagement party, and maybe you'll give me a real answer."

He lifted an eyebrow. "I'll do my best."

"Why do you want to marry me? I'm a complete stranger. You know nothing about me. Not really anyway."

"I know a lot about you, little Emilia. You have a penchant for black, or at least have since your mom died. You hate seafood. You love Limoncello. You play the piano beautifully. You had two scholarship offers at music conservatories. Your father nixed the first one, and you haven't done anything about the second. While you think you're in love with Sal, you don't know a damn thing about him or you'd quickly disabuse yourself of that notion."

My brow furrowed. "Like what?"

He chuckled and his full lips curved upward. "I'm not answering that. You can ask Sal yourself. I know he fed you the story about Sarah, but I don't work that way. I want to win you based on what I do, not what he did. Now drink your next shot."

I did as he ordered. "The next question is yours."

"Do you want to play the piano or do you do it because you think your mom would want you to follow in her footsteps? By the way, she wouldn't care. She'd want you to be happy. That's it."

My heart squeezed and I lurched out of the chair, planting my hands on my hips and somehow knocking over my empty shot glass in the process. It rolled off the table, and Marcello caught it before it hit the hardwood floor.

"What do you know about my mom?"

"Answer my question first, then I'll answer yours."

"I love playing!" I yelled, my right eyelid twitching. "At one time, I suspected I was playing for her. When my father refused to let me take more lessons, I realized I was wrong. Playing piano is in my blood. I need it to feel whole."

"Piano, not Sal," he taunted refilling both of our glasses.

"I'm not talking to you about Sal anymore. Now answer mine. What do you know about my mother?"

He scooted back his chair, the wooden chair creaking when he stretched out his long legs, crossing them at his ankles. "Your mother, Ava, was a very close family friend before she married your father. She even lived with us for six or so months while she was doing performances in the States. She actually met your father at a performance at my house. I was young at the time, only five or six, but I have fond memories of her."

A thread of sadness crept through me, and my eyes stung with the urge to cry. I wouldn't, though. I'd shed so many tears over my mom. I remembered her as this larger than life, beautiful, insanely talented woman with a smile that lit up a room. Yet so much about her would always remain a mystery to me. While I wouldn't describe her as a neglectful parent, she always had a wall around her, blocking anyone from knowing the real her.

"Thinking of my mom makes me sad."

"Why's that?"

"Because I'll never get the chance to know her."

"What do you mean? She didn't die until you were thirteen or so."

"Honestly, we didn't spend much time together outside of her teaching me to play the piano." I swallowed hard. I had no clue why I admitted this. I didn't want him to pity me or think poorly of my mother. In spite of all that, the confession rolled off my tongue like I had guzzled a truth serum instead of two shots of Sambuca. "She delegated the rest of the stuff—homework, learning to read, doctors' appointments, teaching me Italian—to my father, a nanny, or tutors. I guess she had more important things to do with her time than hang out with a dumb kid."

As soon as the last words left my mouth, my chest constricted again, and I looked away, not wanting to see his reaction.

His finger glided beneath my chin, and even with my lowered gaze, I could see him. "Ava's choices had nothing to do with you. She..." He raked his teeth over his bottom lip like he was searching for the right words.

"She what?" I prompted. Nobody around me talked about her anymore except to compliment her talent, and I was curious how people saw her.

"She was impulsive. She made choices without thinking about the consequences."

"You mean like swallowing a bottle of pills after a fight with my dad?"

"Well, yeah, but not only that. She caused a lot of friction within the Families by running off with your father. They were both engaged to other people. It was a mess that didn't end with them."

He grabbed my hands and pulled me onto his lap. I squirmed for a second, uncomfortable with the feeling of his warm hands on my legs. I gave in, though. I'd been fighting everything and everyone for so long, I wanted to let someone else take control until I figured out my next move.

"Did you like her?" I whispered into his chest.

"As much as a five-year-old can like an adult. She made cookies for me a couple of times and tried to teach me piano once or twice. I banged on the keys, and she quickly declared that I didn't have any talent."

The alcohol seeped into my system more and more, and each blink became longer and longer. I was taken aback by how right and wrong it felt to be held in his arms. "Maybe she would have wanted me to marry you."

He scooped me up and came to his feet.

"What about the rest of the shots?" I asked.

"We'll get to it another day."

My inhalations became shallow and rickety. He pulled me into his chest, and his fingers smoothed over my hair. I inhaled his spicy cologne mixed with the hint of licorice on his breath. A rumble of something that sounded like approval rippled from me. He lay down on my bed, his body curled around my mine.

"We're going to be fine, Emilia. I know you're scared, and you don't understand what's going on, but I'm asking for your trust." The tone of his voice webbed around me, evoking a surprising longing deep inside of my bones.

"What's 'fine' look like in your opinion?" I mumbled into his chest, listening to the solid hammering of his heart.

"Come to Chicago for a year. We'll spend time together and if either of us wants to back out, we can. No hard feelings. No marriage."

"A year doesn't sound unreasonable."

He chuckled, and the smoky sound made me hold him tighter. "Glad you agree. So no running. No tricks."

"Hmm." I nuzzled into his neck and willingly succumbed to the siren call of his voice and the lure of his warmth. He clouded my judgment, distorting my desires, my goals, and my future.

"Is that a yes?"

"Yes. I promise," I answered, needing and wanting to agree more than I'd ever wanted in my life. I felt too relaxed and too cherished to do anything except agree, all things I hadn't experienced much of since my mom died.

A spark of hope ignited inside of me. Maybe I could do this with Marcello for real. Maybe he could be what I needed. Either way, I knew no matter where or with whom I ended up, this night, this moment, would alter the course of my life.

"You won't regret this." His mouth sought mine, hot and needy, devouring me in a way that robbed of me all thought, and I didn't mind it one bit. Because in all honesty, an increasingly vocal part of me wanted Marcello.

CHAPTER THIRTY-FIVE

Marcello lifted my dress over my head. Next went my black lace bralette. My nipples hardened, and I wasn't sure if it was a reaction to the chilly air or his heated stare. An image of the curvy Sarah from our engagement party flickered through my mind, and I covered my chest, feeling more than a little self-conscious.

"Stop." He pushed my hands away and cupped my breast, squeezing it reverently, erotically. "There's no reason to hide from me. You're beautiful. Sexy."

"What are you doing?" I murmured, my voice rickety, and my heart doing summersaults.

"We're sealing our deal." He trailed a warm hand up the inside of my thigh, pausing at the lacy hem of my panties. My heart thudded violently. My breaths became ragged. Waiting. Anticipating.

His eyes never breaking contact with mine, he tugged the flimsy material to the side. He glided a finger over my aching center, unhurried and confident, teasing me. Warmth spread from my core to my limbs. I arched my hips and curled my hands into his shoulders, wanting more.

Like he heard my unspoken plea, he dragged my panties down my legs and pushed a finger inside, filling me. I whimpered, and his lips crashed against mine, swallowing the sound. His tongue swept inside, mimicking the rhythm of his finger. In, out, then one finger became two. My sex clenched like it couldn't bear the idea of him stopping. It felt good. Too good.

Marcello's lips slid across my cheek, and he nipped my ear with his teeth. "Has Sal touched you here? Has he done this?"

I considered lying for a second, then I changed my mind. Lies didn't have a place between us anymore. "Once."

He pulled his hand away from me, and my body throbbed with a surprising emptiness. "What else did you let him do?"

"Nothing." Taking in the tic in his lower jaw, I swallowed hard. "It didn't feel right after I met you. I just couldn't."

A shiver of vulnerability trickled through me. Part of me regretted my confession and another part of me was relieved. First with his letters, then with his patience, Marcello wormed his way into my life, and maybe even my heart. Piece by piece, I forgot about my plans for the future, and the moments I spent with Sal felt like a figment of my imagination.

"That's because since the minute I caught you in the hallway outside your dad's office, you were mine, and you knew it in here." He pressed his palm to the center of my chest.

Not giving me the opportunity to refute him, he consumed my words with his lips like he could taste them and his fingers started moving again. Heavy breaths and muted noises filled my room. Every swipe and curl of his finger sent me higher and higher.

I pushed off his jacket and fumbled with a few buttons on his shirt before he took charge and did it himself.

His lips traveled down my neck to the slope of my breast, sucking, nibbling. A groan tumbled from somewhere deep inside of me. In another time or place, my reaction would have embarrassed me, but I lacked the wherewithal to think about it. We were merely two humans cloaked in the shadows, burning up with desire.

I cupped the back of his head, his hair like silk between my fingers, and his stubble like an aphrodisiac against my already tingling skin. I lost track of time, where we were, everything except him and the rollercoaster of sensations rushing through me.

The hiss of his leather belt and the buzz of his zipper followed by the swish of his pants as they swept down his legs echoed through the room. My heart frantic and my mind whirling with the consequences of going any further, I wavered for a second. Something egged me on, though, and I wedged my hand between our bodies, gripping his hard length timidly. He was big. Bigger than I would have imagined if I had thought about it prior to this second.

I rubbed my index finger over the tip in unhurried loops, and I felt him pulse. A hushed growl broke from his lips and he buried his face next to my neck, batting my hand away. Seconds later, the thick, blunt head of his erection was against my entrance.

"Wait," I mumbled, reservations and fears hitting me square in the chest. It would hurt, but even worse, there would be no going back. "I'm not so sure this is a good idea. I mean how…"

"Shh, little Emilia." His thumb circled my clit over and over. The corners of my eyes watered and greedy tremors vibrated my sex. My hips arched off the bed, and my hands clawed at the sheets, seeking the infuriatingly elusive orgasm shimmering right outside of my reach.

He cupped my backside, and his hips flexed forward, nudging his tip inside me. "Still want me to wait?"

"No. Please. I want to do this." The throaty sound of my voice, the conviction in my words, stunned me, but I didn't have long to ponder it.

Marcello's teeth grazed my bottom lip, and he raised my hands next to the headboard with one hand, entering me inch by inch, my softness yielding to his rigidity. His ocean blue eyes clouded with pleasure or lust. I didn't know which. His lowered lashes cast shadows on the sharp angles of his cheekbones.

I tucked my face against the firm muscles of his chest, concentrating on the mini ripples of pleasure instead of the burn. When he was fully seated, he lifted my knees and spread my legs wider. Beat after beat passed without either of us moving.

"Are you okay?" he asked, his words fuzzy like the Sambuca had gone to his head.

Grinning, I whispered into his ear. "Better than okay. What about you? Does it feel good?"

He raised his head, and our gazes locked in a raw, primal dance that made my heart race double time.

"Good doesn't cover how this feels, little Emilia."

I hummed in agreement, all my fears slipping away like they never existed in the first place.

In and out, he rocked in a steady rhythm, slowly at first, then picking up speed when I started to move in unison with him. He angled his hips with premeditated precision, and I pawed at his shoulders, so damn greedy for more. For everything.

A warm ache fanned out inside of me, and I tumbled into oblivion, a kaleidoscope of colors exploding behind my eyelids. I contracted around his hard length over and over, my mind erased of everything other than the pleasure spiraling through me. My neck bowed, my teeth clicked together, my toes curled, and a slow, needy moan spilled from my lips.

He mumbled a few words in Italian, and his hands dug into my thighs with enough force to leave an imprint of his fingers. I opened my eyes, needing to see him. I was glad I did. His features were screwed up, his eyes pinned shut. His nostrils were flared, and his body trembled.

He collapsed on top of me for a few moments, our heavy breaths loud in the deafening hush of the room. "God, Emilia. What are you doing to me?"

Bewildered, I licked my lips, terrified the wrong words would come out of my mouth. All of the times I imagined being with Sal, it didn't even compare to the unsettling emotions and sensations unfurling in my chest. I wanted to simultaneously beg him not to leave and rage at him for finding all the chinks in my armor and embedding himself into my life, my thoughts.

He rolled off of me and draped my naked and limp body over his torso. Somewhere in the back of my mind I registered the achy loneliness within me as if I were no longer whole without him.

I counted the steady thumps of his heart. I inhaled his spicy scent mixed with my vanilla perfume and the unmistakable smell of sex. I took note of the way our sweat-slickened bodies clung together. I felt dampness trickling down my thighs.

So many words were on the tip of my tongue I didn't know where to start. I wanted to tell Marcello I trusted him. I needed to let him know I wouldn't back out on my promise to go with him. That I'd give him, us, a chance. That maybe fate came in unusual packages. Instead, I trailed the pads of my fingers over his chest, committing every detail to memory.

"I have to go. Your father won't be happy if he comes home and I'm still here." He scooted out from under me and crawled out of the bed.

With methodical precision, he put back on his clothes, never looking at me, never reassuring me.

Nothing. Every second that elapsed, my chest squeezed tighter and tighter, and I suspected I was about to experience a full-blown hyperventilation.

"I'll be here around noon tomorrow." His metal belt clanked together. "That should give you plenty of time to pack enough clothes for a couple of weeks. Your dad can ship anything else you want, and I'll buy whatever you need in the meantime."

"Oh, okay?" I had no clue why my answer came out as a question. "And I'll be staying with your sister."

"No." He stuffed his arms into his suit jacket and tugged on the cuffs of his shirt so they peeked out of the sleeves. "You'll stay with me. We'll get married within the next week or two, something small. We'll have a big reception this summer when everything settles down."

I pulled the sheet up to my neck, feeling exposed, vulnerable, and a little sick to my stomach. "You said we could take it slow."

"That won't work. You could be pregnant, and after I explain what happened between us, getting married will be a foregone conclusion."

The blood rushed out of my face, and I folded my arms around my waist, confused how we got here. Confused where the caring understanding man went, then it hit me. "You planned this. You tricked me. The shots of Sambuca, carrying me to my room, sympathizing with me, promising me the trial period. All of it was a lie so you could trap me."

He sized me up for an excruciating, drawn out beat, his demeanor and lack of expression rendering my attempts to read his thoughts futile. "You and I marrying has been a foregone conclusion since the second I saw you standing in the hallway outside your dad's office, all sleepy-eyed and clueless to the chaos building around the both of us. Until then, I was pissed off that we were the sacrificial lambs for other people's sins, but when I saw you, something clicked, and I knew we could ride out this storm together. You weren't my enemy. You weren't my punishment. We were going to be each other's salvation."

My mouth opened and closed three or four times in quick succession like a fish out of water. My heart fluttered at his words, and I quickly shoved the little girl inside of me who still believed in fairytales back into the corner. Fairytales and whimsical castles-in-the-air thinking had no place in the conversation. In my life.

"That's crazy talk, Marcello. I don't even know what that means. We hardly know each other."

He brushed his knuckles across my face. "That's bullshit and you know it."

"What's this?" I grabbed his wrist and pointed at his scraped knuckles.

One corner of his mouth hitched up. "Sal and I had a...discussion the other night. Didn't he tell you?"

My eyes widened. Somehow over the last forty-eight hours, I forgot all about their fight. "What the hell did you do?"

"I made it clear I didn't want him sniffing around my girl anymore."

"*Your* girl? Are you serious? When did I become your property?"

"You've been my property since the day you were born, and tonight we made it official."

I pointed to the door. "Get out. I can't talk to you right now. You're a lunatic."

Marcello palmed the back of my neck, pulled me in close, and kissed my forehead. "I'll see you tomorrow." He scooped up my engagement ring from a glass dish on my nightstand. "And make sure you wear this from now on."

I flopped back onto my back when the door closed behind him, giving the tears beading my lashes permission to fall.

CHAPTER THIRTY-SIX

I woke up two hours later naked and alone in my bed with rain pelting against the house. A burst of lightning illuminated my room and thunder rattled my windows. I inched up my headboard, drawing attention to the dull ache between my legs.

My inhalations and exhalations blurred together as the events of the night clawed through at brain. Shots of Sambuca. Kissing Marcello. Peeling off our clothes. Begging him for more. Losing my virginity. His sudden coldness. The declaration that I was nothing more than property. *His* property.

My whole body tensed, and I squeezed my eyes shut.

Please be a dream. Please don't be real.

I peeled open my eyes, hoping to wake up to a new reality. I didn't. With a trembling hand, I cupped my mouth, struggling to contain the sobs inching up my throat.

I couldn't come to terms with what happened or

241

how I threw away my dreams for him in a moment of weakness. After months of exchanging notes and a week of spending time together, I realized I'd made him into a monster for selfish reasons. Painting him in a bad light justified my decision to flee. None of that explained why I practically begged him to touch me, though.

And *Madone*...Sal. My throat clogged mid-swallow, and I pressed the heels of my hands into my eye sockets to block out the image of his smiling face and trusting hazel eyes. What the hell would I tell him? Merely thinking about him with the evidence of my behavior all over me made my throat convulse. I scrambled to my feet, afraid I'd lose the meager contents of my stomach on my sheets. I paced, tugging at the roots of my hair, my thoughts a jumbled blur, and the only solution I came up with was finding Sal.

Maybe if I confessed everything, he would forgive me. We made promises. He was my friend, my confidant. The conflicting emotions I felt around Marcello had to stem from the stress of my situation. I was confused. That was it. Nothing more. It couldn't be anything else. I wouldn't let it be, especially knowing he'd tricked me.

No matter how charming, sexy, or alluring Marcello was, I refused to be my father's puppet, which meant I needed to do something right now or I could kiss my hopes of shaping my future goodbye. I'd be on a plane for Chicago tomorrow and married shortly after that.

With urgency, I rushed to my closet. Within ten minutes, I was dressed in my getaway outfit, tied the rope ladder to the radiator, and flung it out the window, ignoring the steady rainfall and booming thunder.

I had one leg out the window when I changed my mind and ran back to my desk. I slipped on the bracelet Marcello gave me and jammed the letters from him into my duffel bag. Guilt eating at me, I jotted down a few sentences on a piece of paper.

Marcello,
I'm sorry. I can't marry you when everything is based on a lie.
Emilia

I stuffed the pathetic excuse for an apology into an envelope along with my beautiful engagement ring and wrote Marcello's name across the front. If Sal forgave me, I wouldn't come back here after tonight, and I owed Marcello an explanation.

CHAPTER THIRTY-SEVEN

Wind whipped the fake blonde wig around my face, rain beading on the tips of my eyelashes. With every step in the short journey from the cab to my father's bar, my breaths shortened.

I stood outside the employee entrance with clammy hands and enough uncertainty to make me want to crawl back to my house and raise the white flag of surrender. I steeled my spine and shoved the spare key into the lock. I needed to talk to Sal, and this was the only other place he might be on a Friday night.

My gaze averted and my black trench coat knotted tightly around my waist, I made my way down the hall to the main room of the bar. I'd never been here at night, and the sight in front of me made me uncomfortable in my skin. As stupid as it sounded, I didn't expect it to feel or look like this during business hours even though I'd overheard countless details during my spying sessions.

Women in black booty shorts and sheer cropped tops strutted through the sea of men, their trays laden with glasses high overhead. Top forty hits boomed through the speaker system, mixing with the excited voices and laughter to create something resembling a roar. I looked wildly out of place.

Tugging on my wig, I used the brassy, wiry strands to obscure my face while I scanned the packed space for Sal. I stayed glued to the perimeter, praying no one would approach or recognize me. In hindsight, I should have stripped down to my underwear if I wanted to blend in.

I circled the room once, twice, three times, and my stomach dropped. It was official. I had exhausted all of my options. All of my calls to Sal went unanswered. I had stopped by his house, had a taxi drive me by his mom's house, and nothing.

I slipped into a vacant red vinyl booth near the hallway to the private rooms, weighing my options. If I went home, Marcello would show up at my door bright and early to drive us to the airport. I couldn't leave without talking to Sal. He'd been the light in an otherwise dark year. I'd leaned on him innumerable times. I had to find him. If he didn't show up here by the time the bar closed, I'd camp out on his doorstep.

I loosened the belt around my jacket preparing for an extended stay when Sal's unmistakable voice echoed down the hallway adjacent to my booth. While I'd only been down there a handful of times, I knew it led to the VIP rooms. My father claimed they were for business meetings or private parties. After seeing the bar in action, I suspected something far seedier took place in there.

Unsure if I should interrupt him or wait for him to come out, I hesitated until I remembered the exit at the end of the hall. If he snuck out the back door, I might not find him before my father found me. My mind made up, I trod softly along the amber-stained concrete floor, my heart soaring like a balloon with every step. When I identified his location, I flattened my back against the wall and peeked inside the partially open door.

Lettie was leaning against the wall beside a table, her tight red dress barely covering her underwear and her breasts heaving out of the plunging V-neck. Sal stood with his side to the door, his sleeves bunched up and his wavy hair sticking up like he had recently awakened. His suit jacket and tie were draped over the arm of a nearby club chair.

"You know," Lettie dragged her red-polished fingers down Sal's chest, "I couldn't figure out why you wanted anything to do with Emilia when you could have me. I mean, look at her. She's just a kid."

I bit my lip to smother a gasp of disbelief. The excitement I experienced at hearing Sal's voice and finding him twisted into something sinister and ugly. Sal had lied about his relationship with Lettie.

"Keep Emilia out of this." He swatted her hand away. "She's none of your business."

"Oh, that's where I beg to differ."

"Let it go, Lettie. You don't know what the fuck you're talking about."

"Has Emilia figured out you're a spy for her dad yet?"

My eyebrows shot together. What the hell was Lettie talking about? A spy? A freaking spy? That made no sense. Sal was my personal bodyguard until I left for Chicago. When would he have time to be a spy? Something was off here. Very off.

"It's not like that. Emilia and I are friends."

She snickered, a heavy dose of bitterness clinging to each cackle. Her flawless features were scrunched up into a sneer.

"Oh, I *know* it's not supposed to be like that. Tell me, Sal. What would the all-powerful Dominick Trassato think of you banging his daughter? Because I'm pretty sure when he asked you to watch her, he didn't anticipate you tarnishing his princess by sticking your dick in her."

Sal slammed his fist into the wall next to her head. Drywall exploded, showering Lettie's shoulder with fine white dust.

"Back the fuck off. You don't know what you're talking about. I haven't touched Emilia, not like that anyway. We're friends, and she has a little crush on me. That's all. "

"Oh, I know all about being *friends* with you. We were *friends* once and looked how that turned out."

Sal rocked back on his heels and curled his bloodied fist into a ball. "Being with you was a mistake. One that I'll never make again, so don't go shoving that shit in my face. You have as much to lose as me if Pietro finds out."

Stunned speechless, I slumped against the wall, not sure my legs would hold me. I begged my eyes to look away, but they refused to listen, and the scene in front of me only got uglier. Lettie ran the toe of her heeled foot up Sal's pant leg, and bile crept up my throat. Lying pieces of shit, both of them. I couldn't believe I felt even a flicker of guilt over what happened with Marcello.

"Uh huh, except now you've made another mistake. What do you think the punishment for fucking the boss's daughter is? Death? Torture. Hm." She tapped her finger against her ruby red lips, calling attention to the smeared edges. "Probably both, and don't forget about your poor mom and brother. What will Dominick do to them? Your dad's debt will be on your brother's shoulders, and somehow I don't think he'll fare very well in this world."

"You can't prove a damn thing. It'll be your word against Emilia's and mine, and everyone knows you're a liar. Besides, I haven't done a single thing with Emilia that Dominick doesn't know about."

"Oh, really?" Lettie leaned forward, her lips curling up into a cat that ate the canary smile. "How would Dominick feel about the pictures I took of you two at the Christmas Eve party? Emilia on the countertop with her legs spread, her head thrown back, and you with your lips all over her neck and your hand up her skirt? Better yet, how would Marcello take it?"

My heartbeat accelerated, roaring like an engine in my ears.

Oh my God. Oh my God.

I was fucked. Sal was fucked. Wait, fuck Sal. He was an asshole. They all were. He lied to me, Lettie used me, and my father didn't give a damn about me or he wouldn't be plotting to send me with Marcello tomorrow.

Sal snatched her phone out of her hand and flung it across the room. It thudded against the wall and tumbled to the cement floor. "Marcello doesn't give a fuck what she does as long as she walks down the aisle and says I do."

"That's interesting, because he certainly put on a good show at their engagement party. So much so that you ran out of there like your ass was on fire when he kissed her. And the way, his eyes followed her everywhere. That was pretty impressive if you ask me. If he was acting, he should audition on Broadway. I heard all about this too." She brushed her hand over the bruise at his cheekbone. "Pietro couldn't stop talking about how Marcello kicked your ass. But what do I know about men? I mean, I'm married to an asshole, and you stopped giving me the time of day so long ago I can hardly remember what it was like for a man to give a shit about me."

"That's right. You don't know shit. This whole thing is about money. One-half of the Bonaccorso estate, which will be Emilia's when the old man kicks the bucket."

Her mouth fell open. "Seriously?" Sal nodded. "What does this have to do with you?"

"I haven't done one thing with Emilia that Dominick doesn't know about. Think about that." He tapped his fingers against Lettie's forehead. "Why would Dominick assign me to be his daughter's companion? A guy not much older than her. A guy she showed an interest in."

"How would I know what goes through that sadistic bastard's head?"

"Dominick hates the Masciantonios, and he hates the idea of them ending up with all that money. He blames them for Ava's death."

"Yeah, so? Emilia doesn't want to marry that guy. He should go tell them to pound sand. What can they do? Put a gun to her head?"

"Not unless he wants to risk going to war with the Masciantonios and the Bonaccorsos."

"Who in the hell are the Bonaccorsos?"

"Ava's family in Italy. She went by her stage name to distance herself from them. They're one of the most powerful families in Sicily. She…"

What? My vision narrowed, and nothing Lettie or Sal said penetrated my brain. How come I didn't know the truth about my mom? I always assumed she was an outsider, but she wasn't. She was like me, the daughter of a powerful mobster who only wanted freedom. And that day in the park when that man mentioned the Bonaccorsos…Holy shit, no wonder my dad freaked out.

Sal's voice snapped me back to the present. "Dominick thinks there's a loophole, and that's where I come in."

Laughter exploded from Lettie's mouth. "Oh my God. So you're prostituting yourself and pretending to be interested in Emilia so, what? She refuses to marry that guy? She takes off? She gets pregnant? Tell me, what voids the whole agreement? What's the end plan?"

My chest squeezed so hard it felt like everything

inside was being sucked into a black hole and replaced with pain, anger, and so much betrayal. My vision spun and I splayed my hand on the wall to catch my balance.

Sal tipped his head to the ceiling. "If she marries me without her father's consent, Dominick thinks the Bonaccorsos will back down."

Lettie's laughter came faster and harder. "Oh my God, and you volunteered to sacrifice yourself? Is this your grand plan to pay off your family's debt to the Trassatos? You marry awkward Emilia and voila, your problems are solved?"

"Shut the fuck up, Lettie." Sal yanked on the collar of his shirt like he couldn't breathe. I hoped he fucking suffocated, and I wished she choked on her spit. "I should have never said anything about this to you. Dominick will cut out my tongue if this gets back to him. And it's not like that with Emilia. I care about her."

What. In. The. Actual. Fuck?

He cared *about me?*

I had lived a sheltered life, not by choice but due to circumstances beyond my control. Even I knew you didn't manipulate people you loved or cared about. I stood rooted in place, unable to do anything other than watch the tragedy of my life unfold in front of me.

Lettie's lips still twitching, she tugged on Sal's shirt, and my stomach twisted. "C'mere baby. I'll make it all better. Now that I know why you've been avoiding me for months, I won't hold it against you."

Part of me wanted to charge into the room and

scream, yell, and claw at both of them until they were bleeding on the outside like I was on the inside. I balled my hands in anticipation of doing exactly that, then Lettie's fingertips skidded across Sal's heavily stubbled jaw, and all the fight seeped out of me. Nothing I did would change Sal's feelings for me. I had to face the facts. My father had crafted this illusion to manipulate me for money. Jesus, if he had told me about it, I would have gladly given him what he wanted.

Inching backward, I covered my mouth to ward off the bile crawling up my throat with a vengeance. I'd heard enough to get the gist of what had been happening over the last year. I was a pawn in a game where I didn't know the rules or the players, which left me with one option. I needed to get the hell out of New York tonight and away from all the people who didn't care about me. Who saw me as a cardboard cutout without real feelings or emotions.

When my back hit the cold metal of the rear exit door, I pushed it open and took off down the street, running as fast as my trembling legs would go. My duffel bag pounded an erratic beat against the back of my thighs and my wig swung around my face. I stopped a few blocks away, bent over, and lost my pathetic excuse for a dinner along with the shots of Sambuca.

As I wiped my face with the back of my hand, a taxi barreled down the street and I stumbled off the curb, my hands waving frantically.

The driver pulled over and I climbed in the back.

"The bus station on 8th Ave," I said, short-winded.

EMILIA

When he pulled into traffic, I popped the sim card out of my phone and tossed it out of the window along with all the burner phones Sal gave me. They probably had a tracking device on them, and I had no intention of being found until I was good and ready.

EPILOGUE

After a year and a half of moving from town to town, living in motels, renting random rooms, I found a place to call home. An ad in a local newspaper advertised a position for cooking and light cleaning that included room and board.

I almost didn't bother showing up for my interview because I couldn't take any more rejection. I was numb to everything and everyone, and I wanted to die. I had less than five dollars to my name. I had pawned the bracelet Marcello gave me two months earlier to fix my piece of shit car. The rent was due at the end of the week, I hadn't worked in three months, and not for lack of trying. There weren't a lot of jobs that paid in cash under the table.

Something forced me to keep going that day, though, and I climbed into my car. I promised myself if the job didn't work out, I'd crawl back home, tail between my legs, and beg my father for his forgiveness rather than killing myself like my mom.

An hour later, I pulled up to the gates of a cattle ranch in the mountains of Colorado. Everything about the place took my breath away. Snowcapped mountains framed acres of rolling hills, cattle and horses roamed free, and smack dab in the middle was a sprawling two-story log home. The whole thing belonged on the cover of one of those outdoors magazines. Best of all, it was the polar opposite of everything I'd come from.

The rustle of the wind filled my ears instead of honking horns. Bright blue sky stretched out in every direction without a single building marring the horizon. It smelled of pine needles and fresh, clean air rather than exhaust and whatever restaurant was nearby. I loved it on sight. To my utter disbelief they hired me on the spot, and I gained a makeshift family in the process.

***

Gavin, my best friend and the son of the woman who owned the ranch, cracked open the door to my bedroom. "We need to talk."

My shoulders sagged with defeat. I already knew what was coming. I managed the books and paid the bills. While the ranch wasn't all that profitable in a good year, his mother's medical bills were bleeding the Lancasters dry. "Yeah, I figured as much."

He sat on the edge of my bed. "We can't afford to pay you anymore."

I swallowed but the action failed to do anything about the cotton building inside of my mouth. "Can I stay here for a couple of weeks until I find a place to live?"

"Of course. You're welcome to stay as long as you need. I'm renting out your studio on the first of the month for extra income, but there's plenty of room in the main house. We'll come up with something."

I lived in the studio apartment over the two-car garage, coming and going when I wanted and doing a million and one odd jobs for Gavin and his mom. It was the first time in years I felt like I had a real home, and now it was all gone.

"How bad is it? Are you going to lose the ranch?"

Gavin strummed his fingers on his jean-clad legs. "Nah, nothing that bad. I'm taking out a second mortgage on the ranch. That should cover most of her medical bills. After that…"

His voice trailed off because he didn't need to finish his explanation. His mom's cancer was terminal. The weekly trips to Denver for treatment never managed to halt her decline, and no one, including her doctors, believed she'd make it more than a couple of months.

I covered my mouth, holding in all the emotions bubbling inside of me. I was losing the only family I had. Losing the woman who had become more of a mother to me than my own. Losing the only place where the shadow of the Trassato name didn't hang over me.

Gavin pulled me into a hug, and I smelled that scent of hay and soap that always clung to him. "Hey, don't cry, sweetheart."

I squirmed out of his arms, not able to cope with

the fact that this wonderful man who was like a brother to me wouldn't be in my life anymore because I didn't have it in me to drift from town to town living like a ghost. I had to go home and face my father. "Can you give me a minute alone?"

"Not happening. My mom would kick my ass if I left you by yourself. Now why don't you tell me what's wrong and we can talk about options? Preferably ones that don't include you soaking the bedding with tears."

I wiped my face with the back of my hand, likely smearing mascara down my cheeks. "You wouldn't believe me anyway."

"Give me a try."

"You really want to know?"

"I do."

I cocked an eyebrow, already feeling better with Gavin sitting next to me. He was so unlike Marcello, Sal, and my father. With his golden hair, blue eyes, dimples, and open smile, he reminded me of sunshine and happiness. "If you tell anyone, I'll have to kill you."

He lifted his thumb and forefinger to his lips and mimed locking them. "My lips are sealed."

"I don't know where to start, but here it is. My name isn't Emmie Tate. It's Emilia Trassato."

His head whipped around. "Are you in trouble with the law?"

"Two years ago, I ran away from my home in New York. To make a long story short, my father is the head of the Italian mafia."

Laughing, he elbowed me in the side. "Like the Godfather? You could've told me to mind my own business instead of making up some crazy story."

"No. I'm serious. Take your phone out and Google Dominick Trassato. There's probably some reference to my disappearance."

He pulled his phone of the pocket of his faded jeans, studied me for a moment, then tapped on his screen. "You're telling the truth." He whistled. "Holy shit, girl. You're family's a big deal. *You're* a big deal."

"Not really. I'm just a girl who wanted a new life far away from all that shit. My father wanted me to marry some guy from Chicago. He's really powerful."

"So you ran because you didn't want to marry him?"

I swallowed, weighing my words. "That and other reasons." A pang shot through my chest. God, when would Sal and Marcello's betrayal stop hurting? "Anyway, I've been running for a long time, and it's probably time I went home and faced the music."

"What will happen if you go home?"

"Honestly, I don't know." Memories of the night before I left flooded my mind. "I wish I could find a way to close the door on that part of my life forever."

"Emmie," he threaded his fingers through mine, "will you do me the honor of becoming my wife?"

I scoffed. "Screw off, Gavin. That's not even funny. I don't want a husband. I can get one of those at home."

"That's good news because I don't want a wife."

I frowned. "You're not making sense."

A huge smile split across his ruggedly handsome face. "I'm making tons of sense. Your family can't force you to marry that guy if you're already married to me."

"What's in it for you?"

"My mom's been nagging me to get married for the last five years, more so now that she's sick, and she adores you. I adore you."

I dropped my gaze and traced the circular patterns on my bedding. Gavin had asked me out to dinner almost every week since I started working here. I knew he wanted more than friendship from me, but even after two years, I couldn't get over the betrayal of the three most important men in my life. Sal, Marcello, and my father. They all saw me as a paycheck, and I became collateral damage.

"Then find a nice woman, settle down, and have kids."

"I don't have time for women with my mom so sick and figuring out how to make the ranch profitable."

"Something could change. Maybe they'll find another chemo to try."

Gavin's mouth pulled tight, his eyes dull. "No. She's done. She refused the last treatment."

My eyes widened. "I didn't know."

"She's worried about both of us and maybe if we married..." He swallowed and his Adam's apple bobbed in his throat. "...we could give her some peace. She'd leave this world thinking she'd have grandchildren one day to take over her legacy, because God knows, my brother will never pull his head out of his ass."

His brother Brandon was the black sheep, and in my opinion, he had earned the title. He hadn't done a single thing to help his mom. He made a mess of everything he touched, and he was an all-around entitled prick.

"We don't love each other."

"Maybe with time that'll change, and we're already friends. That's a good start."

"What if you find someone you want to be with?"

"Then we'll deal with it like friends do." He held out his hand. "What do you think? Do we have a deal?"

My heart pounded wildly because, goddammit, I wanted to agree to this stupid deal. We didn't love each other as anything other than friends, but love hadn't given me anything except trouble. My relationship with Sal had been a lie. Marcello, well, I still didn't know what I felt for him except that I couldn't trust him. Maybe friendship was a better foundation for marriage than love anyway.

I took his hand in mine. "Yes."

"We're going to make my mom so happy."

"I hope you're right, Gavin," I whispered as he wrapped his arms around me again.

Five days later, we were married at the courthouse in front of his mom and brother, and I became Mrs. Gavin Lancaster. While I wanted this marriage to be the answer to all of my problems, deep down I suspected it wouldn't be.

***

EMILIA

I was right to be skeptical. My reprieve came to screeching halt nearly two years later when I came home one day and found Gavin with a bullet in his head. With one press of the trigger, the Trassatos took everything. My peace, my new life, my new family. And it was only a matter of time before they came for me, only this time I'd fight harder because I had nothing left to lose.

ACKNOWLEDGMENTS

Thanks much for picking up this book. I had so much fun writing it and weaving all my crazy ideas together with the help of some really great people:

Amy Bustard for reading this book and brainstorming with me.

Chris for helping with too many things to count.

Felicia A. Sullivan for editing this book and giving me valuable, honest opinions.

Limitless Publishing for being so accommodating.

And of course, to all the readers, bloggers, and reviewers who took the time to read this book. Your support and feedback make all the time staring at my computer screen worthwhile!

I'm working as fast as possible to conclude Emilia's story.

ABOUT THE AUTHOR

After spending years practicing law and running a real estate development company with her husband, Lisa decided to pursue her dream of becoming a writer and she must confess that inventing characters is so much more fun than writing contracts and legal briefs. A native of Colorado, she lives with her husband and three children in Denver. When she isn't managing the chaos of raising three children and owning her own business, she can be found reading or writing a book or tinkering in her garden.

Facebook:
https://www.facebook.com/lcardiff11

Twitter:
https://twitter.com/lcardiff_author

Website:
http://lisacardiff.com/

Goodreads:
https://www.goodreads.com/author/show/7692079.
Lisa_Cardiff